Educating Creatures

Part two of 'The Trouble with Wyrms' trilogy
A comedy in three wryggles

Mike Williams

C000161726

DEDICATION

To Simon Nick for his love and support.

Introduction

Not all witches are bad, not all witches have gum disease and a chin like a toilet brush – some witches are just misunderstood. Take the Sisterhood for example, a worthy guild of do-gooders more gin than magic, and more magic than sense. They're neither particularly ugly nor particularly scary. They're just particularly peculiar - a reassuringly, 'maiden aunt' sort of peculiar - wearing tweeds and sensible shoes, but with buttonholes that bite.

Some of the sisterhood are more peculiar than others. There's Arabella Pike, with her cigars and monocle; Bethesda Chubb, with her 'jolly-hockey-sticks' complexion and necklace of dentures, and then there's the delightful Rowena Carp. Miss Rowena Carp – all 'tweed' on the surface and all Vogue magazine in her head; perhaps the least likely of the sisterhood to be given charge of a classroom of smelly little boys, but needs must as the devil drives, and the past teacher of class 2b seems to have driven away as far as possible in the opposite direction.

And so our tale continues. It is time to leave the quiet village of Sodden-on-the-Bog and take the morning train to Grubdale. The rats have gone, the church is still standing and despite the gigantic hole in the middle of the street, life is back to normal with everyone blaming everything on the council. George Stubbins is still serving his cask condition ales in The Lamb and Liver Fluke, Bill Hicken is still drinking them, and Sherlock, his over-friendly ferret, is still eyeing people's trouser legs from under the table. It's as though nothing happened. But not everyone can forget. The Reverend Ainsley Cross hasn't. He's on the same train too, clutching a battered leather briefcase to his chest.

It's best not to stare. The poor man has had a crisis of faith. He laughs to himself and takes a swig of brandy from a half-empty bottle, before opening the briefcase and staring in wonder at the gold sovereigns inside. He could go to the bishop and hand the money over for repair of the church spire, but the option doesn't appeal. He dislikes the bishop. The bishop has a way of sneering and reminding him of all his past failures, of calling him 'Vicar' in such a way that it sounds like an insult. No, for the moment the bright lights of the city beckon, and if not the city, then definitely Grubdale. Grubdale: the most peculiar town in all of Derbyshire - a seaside resort without the sea, where German and English spies sip warm spa water and stare coldly at each other across the bar.

Chapter One

Miss Rowena Carp stood outside the Alpine Palace hotel, sniffed the morning air and felt ill. She hadn't slept well. The hotel bed was lumpy, the town damp and soot-back, and there was this constant feeling of being watched. It was as though the sorcerer's spies were everywhere. Even Demetrios, her beloved pink 'poodle,' had woken up one morning to find his fur combed and fluffed, and with a heap of dead fleas on the carpet. 'Don't look at me,' Rowena had said. 'Your fleas are your own business.'

Poor Rowena; it was her nerves. Today was her first day at school; not as a pupil, but as a teacher at Grubdale Towers. That she'd never taught before, had no idea who she was teaching or what, added to the general feeling of 'Bleh!', of wanting to go back to bed, to sleep and then to wake up somewhere completely different, with a different job, a different dress and most certainly a different mode of transport. Rowena could feel her insides shrink like a walnut. Her carriage to the school had arrived, pulled by a horse of such age and appearance, even the glue factory down the road had waved it past for fear of losing business.

'There must be some mistake,' Rowena said, fighting the urge to scream and take the next train back to Scotland. 'I'm waiting for a cab. The school promised they'd collect me from the hotel steps.'

'Aye Missus, I'm sure they did,' answered what Rowena presumed to be her chauffeur; an odorous old gentleman given to spitting on the ground and scratching the many folds of his corduroy breeches. 'Them lot at the school promise a lot o' things, but it's me that delivers 'em.'

The old man stepped down from the 'carriage,' a horse-drawn van with the words J. Nadin and Sons, Pork Butchers painted on the side, along with the family crest of a squealing pig, a hammer and a bucket.

'But this is a butcher's van?'

'That's right love, every modern comfort, except if you're a pig that is.'

'Well it just won't do,' Rowena said, poking with her umbrella at the crusts of fat and worse sticking to the woodwork. 'I can't climb onto that, it's covered in gristle.'

'What gristle? There's nowt but best meat in my pies. Ask that dog of yours, he seems to know.'

Much to Rowena's embarrassment, her pink 'poodle' Demetrios jumped out of her arms, clambered onto the front seat of the van and started to lick the upholstery with relish. 'Look, Missus, I ain't got all day. You can ride with me or walk. I don't much care. But it's three mile to the school, and all uphill.'

Rowena reviewed her options and thought better of flying to work. Her mission was secret; to protect a young prince from the evil clutches of the sorcerer, Tarantulus Spleen. Flying was forbidden. It wouldn't do to arrive on the school lawn like a one-woman Wagnerian opera; that would be tantamount to ringing a certain Vermyn Stench's doorbell, and giving him the finger, not that Rowena fully understood what giving the finger meant. It was definitely not the way to order a slice of cake in an Italian café, though – she knew that, at least.

Rowena sighed, and resigned to her fate, threw her suitcase at the old man. 'Beggars can't be choosers, I suppose,' she muttered, and lifting her coat and skirt the necessary height, attempted to step up and onto the van.

'Hands off the merchandise!' she snapped. The cheek of it! The dirty old man had put a hand on her bottom! Before she could twist around and deliver a few swipes with her trusty umbrella, the hand gave a hearty push and Rowena found herself high on the seat but with her nose pressed flat on the stained leather covers. 'Well, I never!' she cried, her voice muffled by the upholstery, and while she struggled to sit up, Rowena heard the doors to the back of the van open, and her suitcase land with a 'squelch' inside.

'Nice bit a pigskin,' the old man said, appearing next to Rowena on the seat.

'I beg your pardon?'

'Your suitcase, very posh. Wouldn't mind a bag like that, myself.'

Rowena squirmed and tried to sit as far away from the old man as possible.

'Suit yourself,' the old man said, then picked up the reins and clicked his dentures twice.

The horse shivered, slipped on the cobbles, but managed to pull the van away from the pavement and out into the middle of the road, sending a breeze of warm flatulence that blew Demetrios' ears back like a poodle in a wind tunnel. The old man chuckled, and clicked his dentures a third time as Rowena searched desperately in her handbag for a handkerchief.

'Funny colour for a dog.'

'It soon will be, if there's much more of that,' Rowena replied, pointing in the general direction of the horse's tail.

The butcher's van continued along the high street. It dodged the trams and other traffic that swerved and cut in front, then left the commercial area of the town to begin the long uphill trek past back-to-back cottages and people staring over mud-caked walls. Travelling behind, but conspicuous in its rarity, was a solitary automobile driven by a red-cheeked, be-whiskered man of military bearing.

Captain Hilary Dashing tightened his grip on the wheel, the appearance of the woman in front causing all sorts of shivers and cramps. 'Damned German spies!' he muttered to himself. 'Coming over here and taking all our secrets!' He had evidence - a piece of paper with the words 'Operation Big Secret' and 'Wyrm' hastily scribbled in pencil, and a gut feeling the sisterhood were up to no good. There was 'history' here – 'flying women' history, with machine guns, dynamite and a dragon – although to be fair to the captain, history wasn't his strong point. He was the sort of army officer who'd put 2 and 2 together and get 1066.

'Put your hat on, Private Oldfield,' ordered the captain, looking in the mirror.

'Do I have to?' called a voice from the back seat.

'Absolutely, it's what a Duchess would wear. De rigueur, or whatever the French would say.' Private Oldfield swore to himself, and pulled on a large black circle of reinforced silk with fruit and flowers, and what seemed like the bottom of a parrot's cage after the cat had got in, sewn neatly on top. The captain looked in the mirror again and shuddered. The disguise was perfect, even down to the faintest scent of lavender and haddock.

'Eyes to the front my good man,' instructed Private Oldfield in a voice like the captain's mother. 'We don't want to run those poor cyclists off the road now, do we?' The captain nodded and after adjusting his chauffeur's cap, reduced the speed of the automobile to a stately pace worthy of nobility out on a drive in the country. The cyclists dismounted to let them pass and from brotherly respect to fellow travellers on the road, one raised his hand in salute while the other clicked his heels.

'What are you trying to do Hans, give the game away? Remember where we are and who we're pretending to be. Now, tell me again while I catch my breath and spit these filthy English flies from my mouth, did that woman in the butcher's van look like those others on the moor?'

'Ya!'

'And did she look like the one who tried to kill you in the broom cupboard?'

'Ya!'

'Excellent! Then we shall peddle in pursuit! These English spies are up to no good!'

And so the peculiar caravan climbed its way through the autumn countryside, the butcher's van at its head, followed by the 'Duchess' with the two German cyclists cursing and puffing and making up the rear.

The old man laughed quietly to himself as he urged the horse along with a snap of the reins.

'Do you wish to share the joke or just sit their snorting like a fool?' snapped Rowena growing tired of the butcher's company.

'Me 'orse is on its last legs, and me van ain't much better, but we're still faster than those buggers behind.'

'What 'buggers'?'

'Look for yourself; they've been trying to catch us up since Grubdale.'

Rowena leant out over the side and looked back along the road, revealing her face to her pursuers. Almost immediately the automobile stopped and the two cyclists ran headlong into the rear. 'Do you think we should help?' she asked.

'Don't be daft, we're winning ain't we? Now 'old on to your 'at, while I opens up the throttle.' The old man retrieved a small branch from behind his seat and tickled the horse's rear. Demetrios' ears blew back a second time, but as far as Rowena was concerned their speed remained the same. The 'race' continued with the butcher steering his van this way and that in the mistaken belief that the car behind was trying to pass, until Rowena pleaded with him to stop.

'What's up? Am I going too fast?'

'No,' she answered from behind her handkerchief.

'Feelin' sick then?'

Before Rowena could nod her head and point dramatically with her finger at the horse's rear, the old man yanked hard on the reins and with a shout of 'Geronimo!' steered the van around a sharp corner and up between two iron gates. He pulled the horse to a stop and turned to face his passenger. ''Ere we are then,' he said. 'Grubdale Towers. I'd best drop you off. Any closer and the nippers'll ransack me van.' He stepped to the ground and leaving Rowena to do the same, retrieved her suitcase from the back.

'Don't bother payin' me, it's on account.'

'I wasn't going to,' Rowena replied, looking on in horror as Demetrios started to lick her luggage clean.

12

The old man climbed back on board and picked up the reins. 'Right then, I'd best be off. Good luck, you'll need it.' He indicated with a nod of his head the path leading up to the school. 'Last time those kids won a prize was a raffle.'

'You seem to know a lot about the school?'

'Aye, well the Cook's me sister. I gets all the stories from 'er. A devil's place this is. I give you two weeks at most.'

Rowena dismissed his comments with a wave of her hand and retrieving her sodden pigskin suitcase from a less than accepting Demetrios, made her way along the gravel path. 'Two weeks, indeed,' she muttered. 'Who does he think he is? To suggest I'm scared of a bunch of horrid little boys - discipline and affection in equal measure, that's the secret,' she said. Yet while thinking on her strategy, Rowena felt sure she was being watched from behind the many bushes that grew along the path. Demetrios growled. 'Now, now dear,' Rowena whispered. 'No need to be scared, although we could walk a little faster. No harm in that, is there?'

They trotted along the gravel path, their eyes staring straight ahead until the imposing façade of Grubdale Towers stopped them in their tracks. It was a monstrosity of a building, a dark Victorian folly of gargoyles, stone crocodiles and Scottish pomp that seemed to promise bats, wall-to-wall damp and endless suits of armour with their price tickets still attached. Rowena hesitated before knocking on the door. 'Oh well,' she said. 'We've slept in worse places I suppose.' She hit the door loudly with her fist and found, not to her surprise that it opened slowly inwards, creaking on its rusty hinges. 'This is too much, Demetrios. One hint of a Romanian prince and we're leaving.' She pushed the door further and stepped into the hall, a dreary, dusty room with a stone staircase in front.

'Hello, is anybody there?' she shouted, but there was no answer.

'Typical, all this trouble to arrive and there's nobody here to meet us.'

A bell rang out from one of the towers, and three figures appeared at the top of the stairs, two holding a stretcher, the third lying on it. Rowena looked on in horror as they made their way slowly down the stairs, occasionally stumbling over the worn stone steps. As they passed, the figure on the stretcher reached out and grabbed Rowena's arm. He struggled to raise his head. 'Don't eat the fish,' he gasped before falling back.

'Miss Carp, I presume?'

Rowena jumped in surprise as a finger tapped her on the shoulder. She turned around to see a tall, thin man in a chalk covered gown smiling at her. 'Allow me to introduce myself, Darkly Withers, headmaster of this worthy if faded establishment. I'm glad to have you on board, and so quickly too. Very efficient your agency.' He glanced briefly at the stretcher disappearing down the corridor and frowned. 'I see you've met your predecessor,' he said obviously embarrassed. 'A most unfortunate accident over a tin of sardines.'

'Will the gentleman be all right?' Rowena asked, concerned this was the sisterhood's doing.

'I haven't the slightest idea, although from the state of his room I suspect not. Still, you are here and he has gone. Hurrah to that.'

Rowena wasn't sure she liked this cold, precise gentleman. He looked too stretched, too pale and too tired with life, as though a single ray of sunlight would shatter him like glass. 'Will I get to see the children today?' she asked.

Mr Withers sneered, then put his long-fingered hand on her shoulder. 'Everything in its proper order, Miss Carp. The 'children', as you call them, are out swimming, or should I say being pulled through a canal on the end of a rope. It amounts to the same.'

Mr Withers stared at Demetrios. 'Is that your pet?' he asked.

'Yes,' said Rowena, 'and before you say anything, he's staying with me.'

'Dear Miss Carp, I would have it no other way. I approve of pets. My own I keep in the school pond. They've been known to strip a leg of ham in less than five minutes, a record I believe.'

Demetrios pricked up his ears at the scent of a challenge, but felt a sharp kick from Rowena as warning.

'Time is pressing, Miss Carp. Allow me to show you to your room in the north tower; a quiet corner of the building where you won't be disturbed. Some of our protégés alas, have a habit of crying at night.'

'I'm sorry to hear that. Homesickness can be a terrible burden on a young boy.'

'Homes, Miss Carp? My boys have no homes to go to. This is a school for orphans. We take them in and we throw them out, what lies between is mere education. Now, if you could follow me, please.'

Darkly Withers walked up the stone staircase pointing out some of the portraits of past boys on the wall. It was a veritable rogue's gallery of the wanted and imprisoned, until by the time Rowena was shown to her room, she was holding her suitcase tight against her chest, and half expecting to be mugged at every corner.

'This is where you'll sleep - rather flamboyant to my taste, but the very best we can offer.'

Flamboyant was not a word Rowena would have used, all the room needed was the shadow of the gallows on the far wall, and the atmosphere would be complete. There was an iron bed covered with a thin quilt of crocheted circles, a small desk, and a sink in the corner above a square of beige linoleum. A series of nails had been hammered into the back of the door in place of coat hooks, while an old worm-eaten wardrobe dominated the back wall. 'It's charming,' Rowena said with little conviction.

'Good, then I'll leave you to unpack. We can have a chat in my study afterwards, over a glass of milk.'

As soon as Mr Withers had left the room, Rowena closed and locked the door.

'So, Demetrios, how do you like our new home? It could be worse, but I'm not sure how,' and as if to press the point, fate had the bed collapse in a heap as Rowena flung her suitcase on top.

The cold autumn winds came early, bending the trees and skipping the unfortunate shopper along the high street. It was barely October, and the giant horse chestnut below Rowena's window was stripped of leaves. This was north of the river, where an 'Indian Summer' referred to woollen mittens and bronchitis in the Khyber Pass, rather than a brief warm spell in Grubdale. Rowena tried to stop her teeth from chattering and pulled the thin layers of bedding up under her chin. She would have a word with the headmaster about the window in her room. A few of the diamond shaped pieces were missing, and she'd woken up with her hair all stiff and blown to the left, as though it had been caught in a mangle.

The bell in the east tower rang seven in the morning and Demetrios barked.

'Okay, I hear you,' Rowena moaned, and throwing the covers aside, placed her feet in a pair of Turkish slippers, wrapped a dressing gown around her shoulders and shuffled across the bare floorboards to the door.

'Hurry up then, if you're coming,' she said. Demetrios needed little encouragement. He leapt down from the bed and rushed across to her feet, his tail wagging so fast and furious that it appeared a pink blur. Rowena opened the door, and the two of them stumbled down the stairs of the north tower to the main landing.

'Good morning, Miss Carp,' whispered a quiet voice from behind. Rowena clutched at her heart from surprise. She spun around and was on the point of delivering a tirade of expletives when she saw the figure of Darkly Withers, headmaster of the school, emerging from the shadows with what seemed like a wooden cudgel in his hand.

'You appear very eager to start the day,' he said. Rowena was nonplussed. The headmaster had a terrible habit of appearing from nowhere and the slow, precise way in which he spoke was beginning to grate on her nerves.

'I like to give a good impression. The early bird catching the worm…'

'Really?' Mr Withers looked Rowena up and down in such a way that she felt as though a spider was running across her skin. 'You'll catch more than an early worm in those clothes. I suggest you get properly dressed before venturing out of your room. We don't wish to excite the boys unnecessarily.'

For one brief moment Rowena thought she was being flattered until she noticed the dull, humourless expression on his face. She shuddered and made sure her dressing gown was securely fastened. Darkly Withers stared at the paisley design for an uncomfortable amount of time, then slammed the cudgel into the palm of his hand as an indication that the brief meeting was over. 'Breakfast is at eight,' he said, 'porridge and treacle, highly nutritious. Until then, Miss Carp.' He dismissed her with a nod of his head and walked away into the shadows. Rowena put her tongue out and winked at Demetrios.

'Should we like him dear, our dusty friend from the chalk fields?'

Demetrios barked in disagreement.

'I thought not, too creepy by half. No nipping of the ankles, though. We don't want to get the sack on our first day.'

Demetrios growled in disappointment.

'I know dear, but best paws forward. Now, let's get you outside or you'll be pestering me all morning.' She strolled down the main staircase like a siren of the stage, chuckling to herself as she impersonated Mr Withers' voice, '...we don't want to excite the boys, do we...' she chanted, waving her hands in the air, '...and you in that tutu too.'

Demetrios scampered after Rowena with more urgency than his mistress was showing. He had drunk the entire contents of a large flower bowl and seeing as he was peckish, had munched on the plants.

'Oh dear! I think the outside door is locked,' Rowena said pulling on the large brass ring that served as a handle. 'Do you think you could cross your legs?'

Demetrios gulped and lowered his haunches slowly on the cold slate floor. The plants had been a bad idea, and not for the first time that morning his stomach went into a spin. He whimpered in a most pitiful manner and looked up at Rowena with watery eyes.

'Oh, all right. I suppose a bit of magic won't harm,' and looking around the hall to see if anyone was there, Rowena gently tapped her fingers on the casement lock. There was a loud 'ping', an urgent whimper from Demetrios, and Rowena pulled the door open. The poor 'poodle', for ignoring the pink fur, forked tongue and occasional puff of smoke, 'poodle' was the best description one could apply, rushed outside and skidded off around the corner.

'Don't go too far dear,' Rowena shouted. 'You know how you get lost.' But Demetrios was deaf to his mistress. He needed a large bush urgently, and some soft moss to sit on.

It was beginning to rain. Rowena leant outside with one hand on the door frame and looked up into the sky. 'Oh come on, hurry up,' she pleaded. 'I'm getting cold out here.' There was a sharp bark of annoyance from somewhere to her left, then Rowena found herself spread eagle on the steps as two small figures ran out and disappeared into the shrubbery. 'Excuse me!' she shouted, but was knocked to the ground a second time as a much larger figure ran past in pursuit. 'Really, this is intolerable!' she complained. 'Obviously manners feature rarely on the syllabus. You there! Lend a hand!'

The figure stopped on the path and turned around. He was a burly looking man dressed only in a vest and trousers and had an alarming number of tattoos covering his arms and chest, with a few designs and doodles around his middle too. 'No time for manners,' he snorted. 'Some idiot left the door open and let two of our boys escape. They won't get far, not with me after them.'

'And you are?' Rowena asked, flushed at the sight of all those bumps and muscles.

'Never mind that, which way did they go?'

Rowena was flustered and found her finger pointing to a group of bushes before she knew what she was doing. The man set off and before long was dragging two sorry looking boys back towards the door by their ears.

'The usual culprits, Mellor and Mildew,' he said as he stormed past. 'Stuffing their faces with berries and mushrooms. They'll never learn.'

'I see you've met our sports master,' said a voice too close to her ear. It was Mr Withers making his sudden characteristic appearance and startling Rowena for a second time. 'Rather a formidable fellow wouldn't you say, our Mr Gammon, with all that ink scribbled over him.'

Rowena declined to answer.

'Apparently in certain circles he's considered a work of art, although I can't begin to understand. All those swirls and doodles remind me of a basket of wool. No Miss Carp, I prefer a softer brush.' Mr Withers' eyebrows moved up and down in quick succession, as though to lend importance to this last statement. 'However, we don't employ the formidable Mr Gammon for art.' The word 'art' was dismissed with a wave of the headmaster's hand, as though the very idea was ridiculous. 'We employ the formidable Mr Gammon for his formidable physical presence. I find him an excellent disciplinarian, a necessity here at Grubdale Towers.' Mr Withers leaned over Rowena's hastily covered up shoulder and pushed open the door. 'If there is one word that defines the very character of this establishment, then it's 'survival'. I assume the agency made that clear from the start. Grubdale Towers is not for the weak of heart. The world has turned its back on our boys, Miss Carp. Whatever we do is an improvement, even if it's to teach them how not to get caught.'

It was morning assembly, and the whole school sat silent in the large hall. At the front stood the teaching staff scowling over their charges, or in the case of Rowena, staring at them with open eyes. Some of the boys were not boys at all, but clumsy stretched out youths. If you overlooked the smell and the way they dribbled at the mention of food, they could almost pass as human. It had been a mistake to smile. One of the pupils, a tall spotty youth, returned the compliment a little too eagerly and was winking at the blushing Rowena and nudging his neighbours.

Darkly Withers finished the brief reading from the Bible and slammed the large book shut. The front row of smaller boys jumped in surprise. Their minds had been wandering, and perhaps the parable of the loaves and fishes was too much to take, so soon after breakfast.

'An interesting story, and what does it tell us?' said the headmaster addressing the boys. 'Surely that a meagre diet is a bounteous feast.' He wiped an imaginary crumb from each side of his lips and smiled. 'A disappointing treatise for some.' He tut-tutted and shook his head slowly in mockery. 'We've had a plague of locusts this morning. They've stripped the bushes of berries and gleaned the lawns of mushrooms, all very Old Testament, don't you think?'

Darkly Withers placed the tips of his fingers together and twiddled them in obvious amusement. 'Mellor!' he shouted, and a boy in the third row jumped to attention.

'Sir?'

'Your lips look purple. Are we to suspect consumption?'

The poor boy hadn't a clue.

'You have the mark of stolen fruits on your face. Go and see matron for a drench.'

Mellor's face turned white. He hung his head in shame and walked slowly out of the hall. The matron's drenches were infamous, a purgative for small boys and a guaranteed cure for colic in a Suffolk Punch.

'And what of our brave Mildew? Where is he? Put up your hand, small boy.'

Amongst the sea of worried faces, a solitary arm stretched out.

'Ah, there you are.

'Tell me, Mildew; do you know the difference between a mushroom and a toadstool? All the most famous poisoners do.'

Some of the brighter pupils in the hall started to giggle, all except Mildew whose tongue was beginning to swell and turn yellow.

'Go on,' the headmaster continued. 'Off you trot to matron and be quick about it.'

Mildew followed Mellor out of the hall, but had to be helped by a few of his friends. Whatever narcotics had been fermenting in the toadstools were now having an all-night party in the poor boy's brain. It was then that Rowena decided Mr Withers to be a thoroughly detestable man. There was cruelty in his mockery, and to think the professor had entrusted the young prince to this man's care. She looked around the large hall for a familiar face, but years could bring many changes to a boy. She only hoped he wasn't the large youth at the back. The fellow was definitely giving her the eye.

'On a final note,' Mr Withers continued. 'I would like to welcome a new member of staff. Miss Carp has joined us as a replacement for poor Mr Clitheroe. She will be teaching you the mysteries of science.'

The boys applauded and Rowena curtsied.

'No need for that,' whispered the headmaster, 'you'll give them ideas.'

Rowena had a free morning after assembly. She relaxed in the staffroom in a large leather armchair and read the morning post, a letter from Arabella, which she opened eagerly.

Dear Rowena

Just a brief note to keep you up to date. We are all sad about poor Bethesda but life and Operation Big Secret must go on. Disguising the Great Wyrm as a giraffe was a mistake. The head keeper at the zoo is getting suspicious. He's down two brown bears and a pond of penguins already. Miss Trout says it's murder getting to the droppings before the keeper, but evidence must be removed. Apparently they're stuffed to the crust with bones. I'm not confident of the disguise. All we need is one good downpour, and the paint will wash off. The Professor says he has a second plan, so heaven help us.

Better news about Sodden. We added a few drops of 'you-know-what' to the water supply, and now everything is hunky-dory. The villagers don't remember a thing. They're blaming the hole in the road and the cracked spire on subsidence, and the rats on the council. No sign of the vicar, we may have to keep an eye out there for trouble.

Well dear, how are things at school? It must be strange seeing the prince. Break the truth to him gently. We don't want a nervous wreck on our hands. Will write again soon when I have time. Destroy this letter as the others. We don't want any more mishaps.

Your dearest friend and companion
Arabella

'Really, this secrecy is getting out of hand,' muttered Rowena as she gave the letter to Demetrios to eat. 'This is Grubdale Towers, not that awful hotel. I hope we're not being spied on here.'

Rowena waved to a window cleaner, who immediately disappeared from view.

'Bugger!' swore Private Oldfield, 'I nearly blew it then.'

Chapter Two

A fight had broken out on the school lawn, not between any of the boys or, heaven forbid, their masters, but between two window cleaners intent on knocking the stuffing out of each other. Mr Gammon had been sent out to deal with the situation, but the brawl had gotten out of hand. The cleaners were flailing their tin buckets like two spinning tops, and twice the sportsman had caught a nasty rap on the shins. He limped around the pair, waiting until they tired, puzzled as to what the fight was all about.

'Come on you two, there are enough windows here to keep you both happy.'

The cleaners ignored him. 'English pig-dog!' cried one after being hit squarely on the jaw with a bar of soap. 'Filthy swine!' shouted the other.

'Well make up your minds,' Mr Gammon protested, but it was soon apparent the insults were not for him. The two cleaners dropped their buckets and wrestled each other to the ground, rolling over and over on the lawn as they tried to throttle each other into submission.

'I've had enough of this,' Mr Gammon muttered, rolling up his shirtsleeves and spitting on his knuckles. 'One of you is going to end up hurt if you don't stop this nonsense.'

The tattoos should have been a warning, especially the one of a chicken being throttled. Men who sport such designs tend to bend iron bars as a hobby, or crack walnuts in their armpits at Christmas. Mr Gammon grabbed one of the cleaners by the back of the collar and flung him aside like a spent match, and then turning on his opponent, delivered a kick to the groin that could be felt in the next county. The unfortunate gentleman sat bolt upright and assumed a startled expression, as though he had a mouth full of marbles and needed to spit them out.

'Don't say I didn't warn you,' Mr Gammon said, offering the distraught cleaner a helping hand. The man merely stared back and hissed a few words, 'I'll just sit here for a while if you don't mind,' being the kindest translation. Mr Gammon shrugged his shoulders and turned to the other cleaner on the ground. 'Who do you think you are? Tweedledum and Tweedledee? A fine example you make for our boys, fighting in the open like a couple of farm dogs.'

The cleaner raised his hands in defence then, thinking the better of it, lowered them in front of his trousers. 'Just a silly tiff, that's all, nothing to get worked up about. I'll just pick up my bucket and get going.'

Mr Gammon looked on as the poor man rushed around the lawn picking up a ladder and bucket and waving and bowing in the process. 'It's nothing really,' the cleaner said, backing away from the sports master and making poor work of balancing the ladder on his shoulder. He looked at his watch. 'Well, would you believe it, 10 o'clock already? So little time and so much to do.' He bowed once more then turned and ran stumbling out of the school grounds.

Mr Gammon scratched his head. Typical, he thought, leaving a job half-finished. There was a groan from behind as the other cleaner got to his feet. Mr Gammon felt sorry for the man. He picked up a bucket and chammy leather from the grass and handed them over. 'No hard feelings, but one of you was about to kill the other, and we can't have that, now, can we?'

The cleaner nodded then held on to Mr Gammon's shoulder as he tried to straighten up. The tattooed brute was right. It would be some time before he had any hard feelings down there if any at all.

Mr Gammon walked the cleaner around the lawn till the colour returned to his cheeks. 'Look on the bright side,' he said. 'The job's all yours. If you stay here I'll get one of the boys to come out with some hot water.' The cleaner tried to smile but doubted a bucket of water would do the trick. What he needed was a warm butter poultice and a week's rest. His German masters would have to wait. Private Oldfield on the other hand, was waiting for no one. As soon as he had left the school grounds and had thrown the ladder and bucket in a ditch, a hansom cab drew up to collect him.

'Well?' asked Captain Dashing as he opened the cab door.

'She's hiding out at the school.'

'Good, just as I thought. At least we know where one of those dreadful women lives.'

The captain looked closely at Oldfield's face. 'Your nose appears flat,' he said. 'And there's a bruise on your cheek. What happened, did she attack you again?'

'No, but one of her bodyguards did. I was ambushed on the lawn by a man dressed as a window cleaner.'

'My God, these foreigners are a fiendish lot, adopting our own disguise.'

'I tell you Sir, this mission's getting dangerous. There's something going on in that school that's not British.'

'My thoughts exactly Private Oldfield, but we should refrain from jumping to conclusions. Hard evidence is required before we can act. I'm afraid the Ministry are not convinced. My report of the flying machine was thrown in the bin. I won't lower myself to repeat what they thought of the flying women.' The captain was obviously upset. He took off his peaked cap and smoothed down his hair. 'Have you ever seen me take to strong drink?' he asked.

'No Sir.'

'Quite so, and there you have it.' The captain tapped on the roof with his shooting stick and the hansom cab set off towards Grubdale. After a few minutes silence, the captain felt calm enough to continue his conversation. He was a man of strong emotions. To be laughed at by his superiors and have his sobriety called into question, stung, yet he was nothing if not stubborn. Whatever the Ministry thought, fortress Britain was under threat.

'It's as plain as the bruise on your chin.'

'What is, Sir?'

'The word 'WYRM' of course. It was written on that piece of paper you stole from the hotel.'

'What about it?'

'Isn't it obvious? WYRM must refer to what we saw on the moor, that mechanical monstrosity. If the Ministry won't take us seriously, then we must persuade the King.'

'And how are we going to do that?'

'By usual means, of course - stealth and disguise. You need to return to the school and find out what's going on. That woman is our only clue, now the rest of those women have gone to ground. Think about it, there may be documents in her room, pictures of the flying machine perhaps.'

'But I was never any good at school.'

'That is entirely beside the point. I'm not asking you to be a pupil, but a teacher. Leave the details to me. A vacancy on the staff shouldn't be too difficult to organise, and I think I have the perfect plan. All we need is a dodgy sausage.'

'Sir?'

'Oh, don't be so naive. What's the quickest way to render someone incapable for a few weeks work, besides a bump on the head? Why, food poisoning isn't it.'

'You're going to doctor a sausage?'

'Precisely, and what better sausages to doctor than Nadin's Prime Pork Quality. You've tasted the blighters before; they're absolute muck.'

Rowena was beginning to realise what a peculiar school she'd joined. The staff had done little to change her view about middle-aged men with canes, but at least their conversation was entertaining. Take the gentleman who sat opposite her at breakfast - a certain Mr Rufus Doggerel. Everything about him was baggy, from his eyes to the trousers of his ridiculously large suit. He taught English but had seemed more interested in what skills Rowena had to offer than in waxing lyrical about his own, particularly her expertise in the greenhouse.

'Your predecessor, Mr Clitheroe, was an artist of the soil,' he'd said. 'Such green fingers you wouldn't believe. I don't wish to be rude, but he will be sorely missed. There are certain plants most precious.' There had been a twinkle in his eye and a definite touch of her ankle by a baggy slipper. Rowena

29

explained that she was, amongst many other things, a respected herbalist back home, and this seemed to have interested Mr Doggerel even more.

'Excellent my dear. We seem to speak the same language. Put me down for a pound of the smoking stuff.' He had winked at her and tapped his nose, then dived into his bowl of porridge as though the poor man hadn't eaten in weeks.

It seemed to Rowena, there was a lot of winking in Grubdale Towers. It was almost as if the men believed it to be the only form of address when passing a lady in the corridor, or else reaching across the table for the salt.

'So what are you going to teach the little devils today?' Mr Doggerel had asked after finishing his breakfast. Rowena had confessed that she hadn't a clue but that soap had crossed her mind as a possible topic.

'Take a tip from me, dear. Whatever you teach make it useful. All that stuff about gravity and nasty pongs is fine for other schools but not for Grubdale Towers. Look at me, a so-called English master. I teach them spelling, handwriting, forgery and blackmail. The blighters lap it up.'

How quaint, thought Rowena, but that had been at breakfast. It was now some hours later and Rowena hadn't organised her first class. She decided to search the school laboratory for inspiration. But after collecting the key from the staffroom and opening the burnt and stained door, a quick walk around the benches and cupboards revealed little of any interest. There were a few bleached objects floating in specimen jars full of alcohol, strange plants perhaps or else 'things' of a different phylum pulled inside out. Rowena shivered in disgust. One jar contained the preserved carcass of a gigantic centipede, with the added extra of a shrivelled olive on a cocktail stick floating on the top. Thank heavens she wouldn't be here for the Christmas party.

A large glass-fronted cabinet at the front of the laboratory looked promising. It was filled with shelf upon shelf of stuffed birds and animals, and gave Rowena an idea. She would introduce her class to the joys of Zoology; if she could only identify the various creatures. Most were so shrunken and faded by sunlight they could have been anything. Only the school cat had been clearly labelled - a surprised and moth-eaten ginger tom that looked as though he'd sprayed its last on an electric fire. Still, what the taxidermist lacked in technique, he'd more than made up for in humour. At the back of the cabinet was a ridiculous tableau of a small robin sitting on an egg the size of a rugby ball. Rowena smiled, it was a pity she couldn't use it in class, accuracy was everything. No, she would just have to ask her dear Demetrios for help. The 'poodle' was a gifted mimic and its impersonation of a porcupine licking itself clean had been the highlight of the season.

Rowena left the laboratory fresh with ideas and closed the door behind her. Back in the cabinet, the small robin took a cigarette out of its beak and picked up a scrap of newspaper to check the football scores. The robin, its wife and generations before, had been sitting on that very same egg in that very same cupboard, and a little bit of education had rubbed off along the way. Not too much, for evolution is full of dead ends. The bird was looking at the pictures and holding the paper upside down.

Rowena kicked open the door with a tap of her brogue and marched into the classroom. 'First impressions are everything,' was Mr Doggerel's advice, and Rowena had decided to act upon it. 'Good morning everyone,' she greeted in a cheery voice and placed a large wicker basket on her desk. There was a sullen reply from a score of uninterested pupils. 'Oh come now, why the gloomy faces this lovely autumn day?' The gloomy faces looked back and sneered. What was there to be happy about? They were nearly of the age to be thrown out on the streets, and what then? The coal mine, the army, or if their education had been anything to go by, the prison cell? A cheery lady with a wicker basket was hardly going to change the dull certainty of their lives.

'I'm to take you for science until Mr Clitheroe returns. I'm sure we'll have lots of fun.'

It was the worst thing Rowena could have said. 'Fun' was a pin drop on the Richter scale. It was one of those words that went with 'frolicsome' or 'farmyard' but rarely ever with 'sums'. Rowena could almost taste the dislike in the room.

'Mr Clitheroe never took us for science,' muttered one boy. 'He took us for explosions.'

'I very much doubt that,' answered Rowena. The boy screwed up his face, and someone else picked up the challenge.

'Aye, he did Miss, and sex.'

'Who said that?' snapped Rowena, and an angelic if scruffily dressed boy on the first row held up his hand. 'And you are?' she asked, her motherly instincts bubbling to the surface.

'Pursglove, Miss.'

'Well, Pursglove, it's wrong to tell lies.'

The boy looked hurt. 'But I'm not telling lies,' he said. 'Mr Clitheroe taught us about the birds and the bees.'

'Did he?'

'Yes Miss, he did. Especially about the Cook.'

Pursglove was angelic no more. There was a look on his face that would have sent Jack the Ripper scuttling off to a cathedral shouting 'sanctuary'. He burst out laughing and stared back at Rowena with equal menace.

Rowena sneered. 'Very funny,' she said, stepping back to her desk and standing behind the wicker basket. 'Some of you are going to be disappointed. I'm not here to teach you about fireworks.' The class groaned as one. 'What you will learn from me will be far more interesting.' Rowena turned to write on the blackboard, and the boys began to nudge and whisper. They had emptied a jar of large spiders in her desk, and now a few of the creatures were crawling out from under the lid.

'Pursglove, read out what I've just written on the blackboard, please.'

'ZOO-OLOGY,' he said in an exaggerated, deadpan voice.

'Well done. Now, who can tell me what the word means?'

The class were hardly going to fall for that old chestnut. Answering questions led to other questions, more of the same. They stared at the spiders, chewed their fingernails or else looked blank. If the other teachers were anything to go by then this one would soon lose interest and pick up a newspaper. 'Who cares,' said a voice from the back of the room, and twenty desks rattled and banged in agreement. Rowena pressed her hand down on the nearest lid and trapped ten of Pursglove's fingers. 'I care,' she said, 'and so will you given time.'

It was the first skirmish of a war that would last only minutes, and bigger guns were to follow. As Rowena walked down the centre aisle to the back of the class, she could hear chalks drop on the flag-stone floor like a rain of pebbles. How unoriginal, she thought. The old 'looking up the skirt' ploy. She turned quickly around to see a row of faces peering up from below their desks. 'I wasn't born yesterday,' she said. 'Pick up your chalks and sit up straight.' The class did as they were told, but not without Rowena clicking her fingers and her hemline expanding slowly to her ankles. She shuffled towards the blackboard and ignored the scraping of chalks on slates as the boys tried to gain the upper hand.

'Zoology, surely somebody can tell me what the word means?'

One particular bright spark waved his hand in the air. 'Please Miss, I can. It means we're bored.' The boy smiled to reveal a set of less than perfect teeth, and then fought her unblinking stare with his own.

It was time to unleash the cavalry. 'I am very disappointed,' Rowena snapped. 'What can Mr Clitheroe have been teaching you, for you all to be so dumb?'

A tall lad at the back of the class whispered a possible subject that caused his neighbour to blush and squirm in his seat.

'You there, what's your name?' asked Rowena. The boy refused to answer. He was trouble and obviously knew it.

'I asked you your name.'

'It's Squint.'

'Then stand up, please.'

Squint pushed his desk forward and got slowly to his feet. Rowena recognised him as the smiling boy in assembly, although 'boy' was hardly an appropriate description. In a romantic novel he'd be the gardener. She tried to think of what to say besides asking him his age, for surely the lad was too old for school. No thirteen-year-old would look at a women like that, or stand so provocatively. She stared past him at a damp patch on the wall. 'It's rude to whisper,' she said hurriedly. 'Now sit down and be quiet.' Squint took his time returning to his seat, aware of the effect he was having on this strange woman. Round one to me, he thought and lent back in his chair with his arms behind his head.

Rowena's confidence was beginning to fail. She tapped the blackboard with the back of her hand to get the class' attention. 'Zoology is the study of animals,' she began.

'Then you've come to the right place,' Squint jeered. 'Cos we're nowt but pigs 'ere.' Apparently this was the funniest joke ever told. The class snorted like hogs, rattled their desks and generally ran riot.

'Stop that at once!' Rowena shouted. She stamped her feet and stood with her hands on her hips, but the boys had got the upper hand. 'OOO-ERRR!' they jeered and burst into laughter. Rowena gritted her teeth. She could risk the wrath of the sisterhood and frighten the little horrors with a spell, but she doubted the headmaster would approve. 'I shan't warn you again,' she shouted. 'If you don't quieten down then you'll be sorry.'

The boys could sniff out an empty threat in a football crowd. This woman was soft, all wobbles and perfume. 'OOO-ERRR!' they chanted and threw their chalks at the blackboard. Poor Rowena, it was if she was back on the streets of Vivarium, dodging the tomatoes and brickbats. She stepped behind her desk for safety. Considering the possibility of a lightning strike, or perhaps a headless horseman crashing through the window, she picked up a large spider that was scuttling about on the lid and popped it in her mouth. The effect was immediate. The rattling of desks stopped. The jeering ceased, and the boy's eyes nearly popped out in wonder.

Rowena prodded a long, hairy leg back into her mouth and continued to chew. It was quite nice, almost as pleasing as Miss Trout's budgerigar. She chose another three from the

35

selection in front and dipped them in the inkwell for flavour. These were much better. One could even toss them into the mouth like small pieces of asparagus, and while she munched on her sixth and seventh, she noticed the class had gone quiet. She had no idea why. Perhaps the headmaster had put his head around the door on his daily rounds of the school. Still, beggars can't be choosers, as Arabella used to say when pinching the coffee creams from the chocolates. So using a board duster as a napkin and dabbing daintily at her lips, Rowena began the lesson. 'I thought we'd start with a quiz,' she said opening the wicker basket and lifting out the pink and furry Demetrios onto the desk. 'Who can tell me what animal this is supposed to be?'

Demetrios yawned and rolled out his forked, black tongue. He didn't care for being called a 'this'.

'Any ideas?'

'A poodle, Miss?' asked a timid, red-haired boy with an alarming case of spots. Demetrios looked at him in disgust. What was the matter with the lad? Had he never seen a Jellico from the Forests of Tweeb?

Rowena smiled. 'I don't think we should call it that. It may get upset.'

Too right, thought Demetrios, I'm now an 'it'.

'Come on,' Rowena whispered from the side of her mouth. 'Give the boy's a clue. You can be any animal you want.'

Demetrios snorted and stood up on his hind legs. He stuck out his lower jaw and started to walk along the front row of desk lids, stopping occasionally to beat his chest or scratch his armpits.

'Can anyone hazard a guess?'

'It's spotty Bede!' Squint jeered, and the red-haired boy hid his face in shame. But the class took no notice, the woman who ate spiders and her strange pink pet had captured the moment. They looked on in fascination as Demetrios groomed the helpless Pursglove's hair, picking out the occasional invertebrate and crunching it between his teeth.

Rowena was intrigued. Squint had called out the name 'Bede.' She ignored Pursglove's cry for help as Demetrios sat down in his lap, expecting to be groomed in return. She walked up to the red-haired boy. 'What's your name?' she asked putting a kindly hand on his shoulder.

'Bede, Miss,' he answered in a frightened voice.

'And your first name?'

'It's hairy arse!' shouted Squint.

'How many times have I got to tell you,' Bede shouted. 'My name is pronounced Hieronymus!'

So this was what had become of the prince, Hieronymus Bede, last surviving member of the House of Wyrm. It would take more than a bar of soap to scrub him up as king.

'It's a very nice name, Bede,' Rowena whispered. 'And don't let anyone tell you different.' She glared at Squint. 'You seem to be all mouth today, young man. What are you, the big boss? Well, let's see how clever you are. If you can name this animal, then I'll tell it not to bite.' She whistled at Demetrios, who clambered over the heads and shoulders of the other boys and stood on top of Squint's desk with his teeth bared. And what teeth they were. Squint looked on aghast as the Jellico plucked a long strand of hair from its back and started to floss. Not satisfied with the result Demetrios unscrewed one of his canines and polished it with a cloth. The creature was enjoying himself. He winked at Squint and held the tooth up to the light, examining it as a butcher would his knife.

'Get that thing away from me!' Squint cried, pushing the desk further back with his feet, but Demetrios merely smiled and drew the tooth across the lid, carving a deep line in the wood.

'All you have to do is come up with a name,' said Rowena. 'You seem to have a talent for that.'

'Please Miss,' asked Bede. 'Is it an ape?'

'Yes Bede, it is. But the question was for Squint. Now I shall have to set him another.'

Rowena clapped her hands and Demetrios screwed his tooth back in place and stood up on all fours.

'I am offering you a second chance. Name the animal and I'll spare you your leg. This time, however, it won't be so easy.'

Demetrios took his cue and shook his head so the fur on his neck stuck out like a mane. Squint breathed a sigh of relief. 'Wait, wait, I know this one,' he cried. 'A pink Pekinese, there, have I won?'

'You're too impatient, boy. I haven't finished the question. Demetrios, whenever you're ready, please.'

It was as if somebody had pulled a cord, and the Jellico had inflated like a balloon. Squint screamed in horror as Demetrios towered over him and roared in his face like a lion.

'Well, have you any ideas?'

Squint fell back against the wall in a faint and with a 'pop' Demetrios returned to his normal size.

'Not so tough now, are we,' Rowena whispered as she helped Squint back in his seat. 'Still, you guessed right, pink Pekinese it is.'

The lesson had been a roaring success. Save for a sullen Squint who now eyed Rowena with a mixture of fear, admiration and perhaps something else, the class had hung on to Rowena's every word as though it was gospel. In the hour before lunch the boys had learnt the names of a host of different animals, including a few that were new to science but as common as a sparrow in the forests of Tweeb.

'Congratulations, Miss Carp. I hear you were a triumph,' said Rufus Doggerel rolling up a large cigarette in the staffroom. 'I should be jealous if I cared. Although not all of us have a pet we can bring to the classroom.'

'Damn it, Rufus, but you're not smoking that filthy muck in here again, are you?' asked Mr Gammon from behind a copy of the Racing Times. 'You know how the smell of it starts old Gartside off on one of his singsongs.'

Mr Gartside took the boys for Evaluation, a peculiar subject that consisted of a long line of hoodlums handing over trinkets from their Saturday afternoon trips to town.

Mr Doggerel put his tongue out, and happy that Mr Gammon was ensconced behind a newspaper, offered his bag of tobacco and cigarette papers to Rowena.

'Last of the 1910 harvest, surely a bounteous year.'

Rowena declined and chose one of her own cigars from her handbag, a small black cheroot that was safer than the others she carried. She snapped her fingers without thinking and both Mr Doggerel's cigarette and her own lit up.

'Heavens but my mind isn't what it was,' Mr Doggerel exclaimed, and looked in surprise at the end of his cigarette. He shrugged his shoulders and began to smoke. 'So Miss Carp, or may I call you Rowena? What do you think of our beloved Alma Mata, hardly Eton is it?'

'Oh I don't know, I'm quite full, thanks all the same.'

Mr Doggerel seemed confused and looked again at the end of his cigarette. Even Mr Gammon stuck his head around from behind the paper and frowned. But Rowena was oblivious and lay back in her chair, blowing smoke squares at the ceiling. 'Tell me about the boys,' she asked after a while. 'They seem a dispirited lot.'

'So they are Rowena, so they are. We try our best with the funds we have, but the rewards are few.'

'But what happens to them when they leave?'

'Ah, well that would be telling. Let us say their chances of survival in the outside world are all the better for their stay at Grubdale Towers. Mr Withers would be the person to ask. He's a member of our Old Boys Society.'

'Otherwise known as 'The Firm',' piped up Mr Gammon.

'Okay Jack,' remonstrated Mr Doggerel. 'There's no need to be so honest.'

'The Firm?' asked Rowena.

'An influential body that provides much-needed funds for the school, and protection too. We would do well to change the subject. It is a staffroom rule not to talk about politics, religion or where the next pay cheque comes from. Mr Withers doesn't like it. You see, how can I put it, The Firm is somewhat outside the law.' Mr Doggerel looked agitated. He leant across to a small table and examined the contents of a silver teapot. 'Would you like a cup of tea? I've asked the Cook to spice it up with some navy rum, on account of the weather, you understand.'

'And his liver,' interrupted Mr Gammon putting down his Racing Times and holding out a cup.

'Dear Jack, what would we do without your sense of humour? Quite the comedian you are, and that's a fact.'

Rowena helped herself to a sugar cube and stirred the delicious amber liquid in her teacup.

'There was a boy in my class today called Bede, a quiet, retiring lad.' Rowena sipped her tea, the hot rum slipping down her throat and warming every tiny space of her insides. 'I do hope he's not being bullied,' she said.

'I expect he is,' answered Mr Doggerel. 'All the boys have been bullied at some time or other, even Squint or Pursglove. Mr Withers sees it as an essential part of their education, for when they have to fend for themselves.'

'I think it's barbarous.'

'Of course it is. What do you expect? We're a workhouse with books, and most of those are overdue from the library. Survival is everything, as the great Darkly Withers never forgets to tell us when dishing out the monthly coppers.'

'But Bede isn't just any boy.' Rowena bit her tongue to stop from saying any more. She was a chatterbox on the plonk.

'What's all this about Bede? If he's the same boy I'm thinking of then don't be taken in by his quiet manner. There's poison there; it oozes out of the pores of his chin. Who do you think volunteers to feed the fish in the school pond? No normal boy I can tell you. He positively shines at the thought of watching kittens and rabbits and heaven-knows-what being shredded to ribbons beneath the duckweed. At least Squint has natural urges, disgusting and plentiful though they are.'

'What do you mean kittens?' asked Mr Gammon.

'I'm sorry Jack, merely my poetic licence getting the better of me again. I'm sure little Tiddles will turn up soon.'

Mr Gammon was not convinced. He swirled his rum tea around in his cup before knocking it back in one gulp. 'Bloody carnivorous fish,' he muttered then threw the cup into the fireplace.

'Come on Jack, this isn't St Petersburg. We place the nice china crockery on the tray, like so.' Mr Doggerel made a great display of placing his cup and saucer down gently, even turning his cup so that its handle was 3 o'clock to the spout of

41

the teapot. Mr Gammon snorted in disgust and jumped to his feet. If it was true that Bede had fed little Tiddles to the fish, then there would be hell to pay. Grubdale Towers would be one boy short. He walked across to the large window and leant his face against the glass. It was only three weeks into the autumn term, and he was letting the school get on top of him.

Rowena felt sorry for the rugged brute. For all his bluster, there was a soft heart that beat beneath his cotton vest. She looked down at Demetrios who was happily chewing on a chair leg, and nudged him with her foot. Demetrios raised his head and growled in protest. 'Don't get tetchy with me or you'll stay outside tonight,' she warned. 'Now go and make yourself useful and cheer up poor Mr Gammon. Pretend your Tiddles.'

Demetrios misheard his mistress, either purposefully or not, and instead of adopting the look of a cute little kitten, and rubbing himself against the sports master's leg, the Jellico wobbled erratically around the room, hiccupping and bumping into the furniture.

'One thing I draw the line at Rowena, is sharing my rum with a poodle,' said Mr Doggerel wagging his finger in her face. 'It is an occasional treat not to be squandered.

'Speaking of treats,' said Mr Gammon staring out on the lawn. 'It looks as though sausages are back on the menu.' Running up the path was the unmistakeable figure of Nadin the pork butcher carrying a cloth-covered basket in one arm and pushing away a host of inquisitive boys with his other. Mr Gammon swung open the window and shouted down.

'Leave that poor man alone or I'll be out there to give you all a good hiding.

'Well, that's one bit of good news anyhow,' he said thinking of the sizzling bangers that would be plump and juicy on his dinner plate that evening. 'You're in for a treat Miss Pike, if you've not tasted Nadin's Prime Pork Quality. They've won medals you know, at all the big competitions. It's as his slogan says – "You can't keep a good sausage down."'

Chapter Three

Captain Dashing had done his work well; a member of staff had taken ill in spectacular fashion.

'Dear boys,' said Darkly Withers addressing the school at morning assembly, 'let us put our hands together and say a prayer for the speedy recovery of Mr Maurice.'

The foolish sniggers of the class were in stark contrast to the solemn faces of the teachers who, sleepless from the night before, were clenching their buttocks, belching and still tasting Nadin's Prime Quality Pork.

The headmaster scanned the hall and recognised the giggling schoolboys at once. He smiled in his own sinister fashion and rubbed his chalk-dusted hands with glee.

'Let us also say a prayer for Mellor and Mildew who, no doubt from respect, have so kindly volunteered to clean up the mess.'

Mellor and Mildew looked at each other in alarm. The smell of sausages from the staff table the previous evening had gone to their heads and they were still giddy on grease. They thought better than to protest, and accepted their fate like the brave boys they were, whimpering and snivelling and looking down at their feet. There were other boys sniggering, but the headmaster's eyes were all seeing.

'It appears Pursglove and Squint think little of this unselfish act. Let us ponder in silence the error of their ways as they make their way to my office.'

A sneering Darkly Withers nodded to Mr Gammon to escort the two culprits out of the hall. As an indication of the pleasures to come, he bent his cane double and flicked at a solitary bluebottle that had escaped from the kitchens. He wiped the tip clean and continued with his speech.

'Mr Maurice will be sorely missed, particularly at assembly. Although we thank the resourceful Mr Doggerel for his tissue paper and comb accompaniment, we look forward to the arrival of a replacement music teacher with interest.'

Mr Doggerel bowed his head in thanks, his lips on fire from a four verse rendition of 'Onward Christian Soldiers' in double quick time.

'However, on a different matter,' continued Mr Withers. 'Cook tells me a large number of fish heads were found uneaten this morning. We're not made of money. Think of all the starving children in the world, and be grateful for small mercies. There'll be fish heads for lunch and I expect each and every bone picked clean.'

Rowena nodded in agreement. Fish heads were a delicious snack, and she often wrestled Demetrios for the last morsel. She searched the audience of green-faced boys and smiled as she made out the red hair and oily complexion of the prince. The poor boy, she thought, a hot bath and a few books balanced on his head would put him right, as would a regular dose of clean, fresh air. She made a mental note to organise a nature walk for her class. It would be something new and interesting for the boys, and would solve the problem of

45

Demetrios having exhausted his repertoire of animal impressions the day before. She was sure the headmaster would approve.

'But Miss Carp, this is autumn. What on earth is there outside to interest the boys?' was his reply later that morning. 'The Season of Mellow Fruitfulness? It's hardly a term I would use to describe the moors in October. The countryside is nothing but brown slush this time of year. As to your suggestion of a 'Fungal Foray'...out of the question. The boys are excitable as it is without recourse to chemical stimulants. No Miss Carp, you would do better to keep them in the classroom and have your little adventure there. There's more wildlife in their clothes than what scuttles about outside.'

It was a furious Rowena that left the headmaster's office and stormed up the stairs to her room. Squint was hiding in the shadows as she passed and was struggling with a new emotion. He was beginning to find the new science teacher strangely alluring.

Rowena lay down on her bed and read the latest letter from Arabella that had arrived that morning. It contained a marvellous photograph of the wyrm taken shortly before the creature had been painted yellow and brown and passed off as a giraffe.

Dear Rowena
Isn't Her Majesty a wonderful specimen?

Rowena had to agree and wiped a tear from the corner of her eye.

I can't attempt to describe how beautiful she is so I thought I'd send you this photograph. Yesterday she greeted the Professor with a loud 'Good Morning.' She speaks perfect English, which has the Professor in a complete muddle. He has some theory about the Great Wyrms teaching language across the whole universe, but I think it rather far-fetched.

The zoo keeper is depressed. The number of disappearing animals is getting him down. He's hearing noises in his sleep now - the crunching of bones and the gurgling of plumbing. I suspect Her Majesty. We shall have to smuggle her out soon, as any more of these midnight snacks and she'll be the only exhibit in the place. I don't know if you've read the papers, but the local press are convinced the town is full to overflowing with wild beasts. One more 'lost' giraffe won't make any difference. The professor is even thinking of hiding her in a circus. He says no one will believe she's an actual dragon, but people will pay good money to see her. Do you think he's short of a bob or two?

How are you getting on with our prince? Have you told him yet?

Your dearest companion
Arabella

Rowena fed the letter to Demetrios and gazed for a while at the photograph. How could anyone be so stupid as to mistake a wyrm for a giraffe? No, she thought, perhaps the circus was the better plan, even though it would be an insult to have her juggling balls on a tightrope.

There was a knock on the door. Rowena got up quickly from her bed and hid the photograph under the pillow. She straightened her hair, smoothed down her dress and called out 'Come in,' in her best schoolmistress voice. The door opened and to her embarrassment a scrubbed and polished Squint stood outside. He was attempting to appear casual by leaning against the doorframe but looked instead as though the room had turned through 45 degrees.

47

'What do you want?' Rowena asked, but for once Squint's bravura failed. He could think of nothing to say that would suggest sophistication with a hint of danger sprinkled on top. He swept his hair back in a devil-may-care fashion, hoping this youthful display would make up for any lack of conversation. It didn't, his nerve broke. 'I've brought Bede,' he mumbled, 'says you sent 'im a note.' There was a note of jealousy in his voice.

'I did, but I'm sure he's a big enough boy to make his own way up the stairs.'

'Just checking, 'case 'e was making it up. 'As a habit of fibbing, this one.'

Rowena found herself both annoyed and amused. 'Whereas you don't, Squint?' she asked. There was something in the way she pronounced his name that made it sound like an affliction. The young man stood up straight in the doorway.

'I'll send 'im in then, should I?'

'Yes Squint, why not do that.'

Squint gave a quick, sharp whistle, and a very nervous Bede appeared behind him.

'Come on in, don't be shy,' said Rowena. 'I thought it would be nice if we had a little chat.' She placed her hand on the boy's shoulder and led him into the room, and with a light tap of her shoe closed the door on Squint. 'Would you like a sweet?' she asked. 'I have a bag of chocolate limes somewhere in the room, if Demetrios hasn't scoffed the lot.'

There was a disgruntled 'harrumph' from under the bed. The effrontery of the woman, thought Demetrios licking the last of a chewed sherbet fountain from off his face. As though a noble Jellico would stoop to thievery; he was merely looking after his mistress's figure.

'Here we are,' said Rowena hunting through her pockets. 'I knew I had them somewhere.' She brought out a crumpled paper bag and offered it to Bede. He thrust two grubby fingers inside and nearly tore the paper apart in his eagerness to get a sweet. 'Perhaps you should keep them all,' Rowena said after noticing his dirty fingernails and the boy snatched the bag and held it greedily to his chest. Hardly the behaviour of a prince, she thought, but then perhaps the poor boy didn't know any better, the trauma of his parents' death and years at Grubdale Towers were obviously to blame. She pulled a chair from out of the corner and beckoned the boy to sit down.

'So tell me Bede, how old are you?'

The boy stopped sucking his sweet and thought for a moment. 'Thirteen, I think,' he said. 'I'm not sure. I can't remember much.' He continued with his chocolate limes and popped two more into his mouth for good measure.

'I don't think that's true,' said Rowena. 'Look how well you got on in my class yesterday. You remembered a lot of names.'

'That's nothing, just animals and stuff. Everyone knows about animals.'

'And Jellicoes?' suggested Rowena, but the boy failed to rise to the bait. He was looking around the room as though the name didn't mean anything.

'Is this where you sleep?' he asked, and Rowena nodded. 'It's nice,' he said. There was another 'harrumph' from under the bed, a feeling shared by Rowena.

'Well, it's hardly a palace,' Rowena said and studied Bede's face for a reaction. The boy stared back and frowned, he wasn't comfortable being looked at so closely. Rowena sighed. To hell with it, she thought, I might as well tell him straight, and never one for slapping newborn babies gently on the bottom, Rowena hit Bede for six by showing him a small painting of his parents.

'What's this?' Bede asked as he was handed a large and heavy silver locket. 'A present?'

'You could call it that, open it up and look inside.'

Bede struggled with the clasp then smiled with delight as the two halves of the locket opened to the sound of a music box. Inside were two miniature paintings, one of a King and Queen and the other of himself. He crunched his sweets in time to the music and felt the weight of the locket in his hand. If this was pure silver then old Mr Gartside would be able to get him a good price. He turned the locket over to check for hallmarks and Rowena caught hold of his hand and turned it the other way.

'These are your parents,' she said after a tactful silence. 'And that's a painting of you when you were much younger.'

Bede looked closely at the pictures trying to comprehend what Miss Carp had just said. Did this mean that he couldn't sell it? 'But they're both wearing crowns,' he said.

'Of course they are. That is King Adolphus the Sixth.' Rowena sighed, stroking the miniature portrait with her thumb and remembering far happier days. 'Next to him is your mother, Queen Potentilla. Don't you think they make a lovely couple?'

Bede stood up and walked across to the small window. He stretched out his arm so that the sunlight fell on the locket, and then scrutinised the paintings, first with one eye closed and then with the other. It was as though he was looking for some hidden key that would unlock his memory.

'But if these are my parents, then that means I'm a...'

'Prince,' interrupted Rowena.

50

Bede turned to face her, not knowing what to think. 'It's not true,' he said, 'someone called George is King, everyone knows that.'

'Yes, but this George is the King of England. Your parents are, or were should I say, rulers of a different country.'

'You mean I'm a bloody foreigner?'

'You could say that, but I wish you wouldn't. Honestly, I despair of this school. Anyone can be a bloody foreigner, even an Englishman. What is important is that you are a prince.'

'I am?'

Rowena knelt on one knee and held his hand. 'Yes, your Highness,' she said.

Bede laughed at his new title and sat down in the chair as though it were a thrown. 'This is terrific!' he said. 'Just wait till I tell the others.'

'No!' Rowena insisted. 'You can't tell anyone, it wouldn't be safe.'

Bede looked crestfallen. What was the use of being a prince if no one knew? Half the fun it seemed was to lord it about and be superior. 'Why can't I?' he asked. 'It doesn't seem fair.'

'You would only be made fun of and bullied.'

'But I am!' Bede cried.

Rowena tried to hide her disappointment, the boy hadn't asked about his parents. 'Please, listen to me,' she said. 'No one would believe you. The bullying would get worse. Be patient, you will be going home soon.'

'Home?' Bede's eyes opened wide with surprise. He hadn't thought of that, to be rid of Grubdale Towers would be the best present of all. 'And where's home?' he asked.

Rowena had been dreading the question. 'Vivarium,' she mumbled as though there was nothing peculiar about the name.

'Never heard of it, where is it?'

Rowena scratched her head and tried to think of a simple explanation, one that wouldn't send the lad screaming down the corridor. 'This is not going to be easy,' she said. 'Let's say that this peppermint is Grubdale.'

Demetrios popped his head out from under the bed and drooled. His mistress' pockets were a veritable treasure trove of confectionary.

'Then where you come from would be about as far away from this sweet as you could imagine.'

'As far away as Africa?' asked Bede, his mind spinning with exciting possibilities.

'Even further away than that.'

Bede was beginning to enjoy the game. Further away than Africa was almost unimaginable. 'You could point the country out to me on a globe,' he said. 'There's a big one downstairs in the classroom.'

Oh dear, thought Rowena, here come the hysterics. 'I don't think that would help,' she said and threw the peppermint to Demetrios. 'Forget about Grubdale; let's say that this orange is where we are. Now look across at the doorknob, that's our nearest planet.'

Demetrios swallowed the peppermint and stared hungrily at the fruit. If Rowena was about to describe the whole solar system, then he was in for a feast.

'To arrive at Vivarium we would have to travel to the North Pole, I think.'

Bede stared at Rowena with his mouth open, a dribble of saliva trailing down to his knees. It seemed an age before he spoke, for he had just seen all his dreams vanish in the back of a white van from the sanatorium. 'You're lying,' he said in a quiet, controlled voice. 'That means I'm from outer space.'

'Don't be so provincial dear. Some of the nicest people are from outer space.'

It was hardly what the boy wanted to hear. 'You're making fun of me,' he cried, standing up from his chair.

'No, I am not. If you would only listen, I could try and explain. This is not easy for me, Bede. I wish Professor Broadbent was here to help.'

At the mention of the professor's name Bede seemed to calm down.

'You know the professor?'

'Yes,'

'He's kind. He visits me sometimes.'

'Does he?' said Rowena, surprised. 'Well it's a pity he didn't tell you this before, it would have saved a lot of time and worry. There's no simple way to say this young man, all three of us arrived on Earth ten years ago.'

'You mean both you and the professor came with me from Viv, Viv…'

'Vivarium, and yes we did, along with a lot of other people.'

Bede's face turned red with rage. 'I don't believe you,' he cried. 'It's impossible, how did we get here, fly?'

'Now you're being stupid. We didn't fly, we walked, isn't it obvious?'

Bede flung the chair across the room. 'You're mad!' he screamed, backing away towards the door.

'Is it my fault you don't understand physics? Grow up boy, stop acting like a child and lower your voice!'

'Get away from me!'

This was too much for Rowena. She flung the chair aside and grabbed Bede by the collar. 'You may be a prince, but it doesn't stop me from giving you a good, hard slap! If anyone is short of marbles then it's you, forgetting your past. Ask yourself this, what do you remember before coming to Grubdale?'

The boy was in hysterics. 'Nothing!' he cried. 'I remember nothing!'

'Then it's my job to see that you do.'

Rowena dragged the struggling Bede to the mirror above her sink and forced him to look at his reflection. She held the locket open at his side.

'Tell me what you see.' she said.

Bede stared at his face and then at the small portrait. What the mad woman was saying was impossible. 'It's not me,' he sobbed. 'It's not me!' But the similarity between his reflection and the image was beyond doubt.

'These are your parents, boy. Look at them. It's bad enough they're dead, but to deny their existence is intolerable.'

'Leave me alone!' Bede screamed. He pushed Rowena away and flung himself down on the bed.

'You can cry all you want, but it won't change the past. You are the Prince of Wyrm, so get used to it.'

Bede thought this the cruellest trick of all. 'Worms?' he cried. 'I'm a prince of worms? What sort of a silly name is that?'

'It is a very noble title. The House of Wyrm goes back thousands of years. You will wear the badge of the Great Wyrm with pride, the symbol of Mathog, of all that is strong and true in our world. And you say you don't remember?'

Rowena waited until the tears had stopped, then sat down on the bed. She felt under the pillow for the photograph of the wyrm and placed it in the prince's hand. 'Shut up you,' she whispered to Demetrios, who was shaking his head. It was a few minutes before Bede spoke again.

'Mathog?' he muttered looking at the photograph.

54

'What did you say?'

The boy snuffled. 'Mathog,' he whispered.

Rowena felt a lump in her throat. She reached out and stroked his hair. 'No my dear, not Mathog, but it's a Great Wyrm none the less.'

Bede wiped his eyes and sat up from the bed. He took the locket from Rowena and began to hum along with the melody. 'I've heard this tune before,' he said between snuffles.

'I know. The locket was a gift to you from your mother. I've kept it safe.'

Bede stared at the picture of his parents, trying to focus through his tears. He grabbed Rowena tightly by the hand. 'Why was I sent here? This is no place for a prince.'

'It was the professor's doing. He thought this school the safest place to hide you. Only the lost come here.'

'But they beat us.'

'That will stop, and the bullying. I will see to it myself.'

'But why here, I don't understand.'

'There's something I haven't told you. You were brought here for your own protection after your parents were murdered. As the last member of the Royal House of Wyrm your life was in danger.'

'Murdered?'

'I'm sorry, there was no easy way to break it to you. The person responsible is still at large. His name is…' Bede covered Rowena's mouth with his hand. Some words were better left unsaid.

'Would you like to be left alone for a while?' Rowena mumbled through his fingers. 'I could lock the door so that you're not disturbed.' Bede tried to say something, but his whole body shook with terrible sobs. Rowena reached out and held him in her arms. 'There, there,' she said rubbing his back.

'You will remember everything in good time.' She looked down at Demetrios and smiled. 'That went better than expected,' she mouthed, but then she couldn't see the boy's eyes.

'How am I supposed to touch the pedals if I can't show my ankles,' complained Private Oldfield, sitting down at a piano. He was wearing a floor-length black dress and a grey wig tied up in a bun.

'I haven't a clue,' said Captain Dashing. 'You're supposed to be the expert, improvise. We could always make the dress longer.'

'I'm tripping up as it is.'

'Then try wearing boots. If this disguise is going to work, you must look the part, and if I remember correctly I never once saw my Grandmother's feet. Even Grandfather said she was a mystery below a string of pearls.'

'Why can't I be a man?' Oldfield muttered. 'It would be much easier.'

'And how exactly are you going to be invited to that woman's rooms, tell me that? There are certain rules you know. It is a school. Now stop complaining and play some music.'

Private Oldfield ran his fingers across the keys and tried to look as though he knew what he was doing. He started in the centre and worked outwards to the edge then raising his hands high above his head, brought them crashing down for the chorus. There was a noticeable pause, about twelve bars as far as the quill scribbles.

'What the hell was that supposed to be, something Russian?'

'I'm not sure, mostly these white bits I think. I told you I couldn't play the piano.'

'And what good is that to me, I've already informed the school you're coming.'

The afternoon had been mostly like this, Private Oldfield complaining and the captain in a panic, for of all the teachers to have picked the dodgy sausage, Mr Maurice was the most difficult to replace. They had argued about the costume, the musical instrument, and Oldfield's new name and the captain had pulled rank each time. There were to be no trousers, no swanny whistles, and definitely no Nelly Deans.

'From now on Oldfield, you shall be known as Dr Hildegard Brent. I'm sorry about the title, but I had to guarantee your employment at all costs. You are an aged spinster of limited means, who would gladly work for half wages if given a soft bed for the night and a cup of cocoa.'

'What?'

'Trust me, it was stiff competition. You nearly didn't get the job.'

The problem of the piano remained.

'I have the perfect solution. All you need do is play the piano in assembly each morning. Bang out a chord to get them started, then conduct the singing with a baton. You won't have to touch the keys after that. Now, cover your ankles and come to the pub. I want to see how convincing your disguise is. Remember, no pints of bitter but a glass of sherry, and screw your face up when you take a sip, it was another habit of my Grandmother.'

Private Oldfield looked worried, what would happen if his disguise didn't work? Grubdale was hardly the place to be seen drinking with a man in a dress, not like the Sudan, or was that a sheik? He only hoped the captain had a backup plan.

The two of them walked through the fog to a hostelry on the corner of the high street where the captain held the door open and guided Private Oldfield through to the snug. 'It's safer in here,' he said. 'The lights are low, and we seem to be the only one's here at the moment.' Captain Dashing rang the bell for service and peered through the serving hatch to the front bar.

'Hey-ho if it's not one of Hicken's heroes. I salute you Sir, and your uniform.'

The voice came from a dishevelled looking gentleman who nodded towards the captain and downed a glass of port.

'Now then you,' warned the landlord. 'Leave the officer alone or you'll be out on your ear.'

'My dear man, please accept my apologies. See, I shall stitch my lips shut like this.' The gentleman smiled and impersonated a tailor sewing with a needle and thread. 'On second thoughts,' he said tossing a few coins on the counter, 'how about another drop of the 'Portugal's'? Oops, there goes the last of the collection money. Have to break into the steeple fund now, won't I.'

The gentleman opened a leather bag and placed a gold coin in his left eye. 'By Jove,' he added pretending to be surprised by his surroundings. 'It's the Bishop's Palace!'

'Don't mind him, Sir,' said the landlord. 'He's just a harmless eccentric. Popped into the pub three days ago and has been visiting us ever since.'

The captain smiled and ordered his drinks.

'Allow me to pay for them,' continued the gentleman, 'as a mark of respect for your rank.'

The captain declined.

'Refuse all you want dear chap, but I've made up my mind. Here, landlord,' said the gentleman throwing the gold coin towards him. 'A bottle of port and whatever your good self is having. No, I insist.'

The coin made all the difference. The landlord seemed transfixed as it span on the counter, then snatched it up and tested it between his teeth.

'You'll find it quite genuine. Now what about some food, your largest pork pie and a pot of mustard I think.'

Captain Dashing shrugged his shoulders; some people had more money than sense. He returned to the corner of the snug and sat opposite Private Oldfield. 'Here's to our mission, Dr Brent,' he whispered and took a large gulp from his pint. Private Oldfield sipped at his sherry and screwed up his face as he was told. 'Oh, well done Dr Brent, that was just like my Grandmother.'

The door to the snug swung open, and the eccentric gentleman stumbled in with his leather bag. 'Do you mind if I join you.' He paused, Private Oldfield's appearance had taken him by surprise and for one embarrassing moment Captain Dashing thought the disguise had failed. He needn't have worried. The gentleman stood up straight and adjusted his jacket. '…and your dear lady?' he said. The captain nodded. If this jovial character couldn't tell the difference, then all would be safe for tomorrow.

The gentleman squeezed himself onto the settee next to Private Oldfield. 'The conversation next door is not what it used to be,' he whispered and tapped his nose in conspiracy. 'Lovely landlord but a little thin on adventure.' He laughed and held out his hand in greeting. 'Allow me to introduce myself, the Reverend Ainsley Cross, but you two can call me Vicar. I seem to answer to that more times than my name nowadays.'

'Delighted to meet you,' said the captain shaking his hand. 'Hilary Dashing, and this charming woman seated next to you is Dr Hildegard Brent from the Royal College of Music.'

A nervous Private Oldfield offered his hand, and the vicar squeezed it, briefly.

'A doctor of music? Then I am indeed honoured,' although the embarrassed look on the vicar's face seemed to tell a different story. He wiped his forehead with an old rag from his top pocket and pulled the sleeves of his jacket over his dirty cuffs. 'You must excuse my appearance,' he continued. 'It is no reflection of the man, merely the bumps and scrapes of an eventful past; nothing a quick flick of a flannel can't put right.' He took the newly purchased bottle of port from his leather bag and placed it rather shakily on the table. 'There, all we need now is some clean glasses.' He rummaged in his bag and brought out three china cups of exquisite taste. 'Sorry about the lack of saucers, I was in a bit of a rush when I packed.' He poured three large measures and licked his lips before taking a sip. 'Cheers you two,' he said as an afterthought, then downed his cup in one.

The landlord appeared with the food, a large pork pie with its golden crust glistening under the gaslight. The vicar wasted little time in cutting himself a quarter, smearing the slice with dollops of mustard and attacking it like a dog with a slipper. He smiled at Private Oldfield as he chewed. 'I too am a scholar of the arts,' he said spitting out a fountain of pastry crumbs. He searched inside his jacket and produced a well-thumbed photograph. 'One of my better portraits,' he explained. 'The Venus de Milo, with Arms.'

Private Oldfield took one look at the image and choked on his sherry. There were legs, and other bits included.

'I've caught the look of innocence rather well, don't you think, although as you can see it was cold in the studio.' The Vicar passed the photograph to the captain who immediately blushed and crossed his legs. 'Of course, I'm only an amateur but I like to think there's promise.'

The vicar continued to eat the pork pie and help himself to the other two cups of port, all the time staring at Private Oldfield. 'You remind me of someone,' he said pointing with a piece of crust. 'If you had red hair and weren't in that dress I could have sworn...' He stopped abruptly, the look on Oldfield's face seemed to suggest some slight misunderstanding, the sort of double-speak that could only be followed by a hard slap and the clatter of dentures hitting the ceiling. 'My dear lady,' he continued. 'What I was trying to say is that in a dark crypt with the light behind you...' The exact words seemed to escape him. 'Oh, damn it all Dr Brent, have you ever dressed up in tweeds?'

'No, I certainly have not,' scolded Private Oldfield.

'Good, I'm glad to hear it,' mumbled the vicar, realising he had gone too far.

'What exactly are you hinting at?' asked Captain Dashing, coming to his companion's defence.

'Only that your good friend here should be more careful about her appearance. It would be most unfortunate if she were to be confused with those other women.'

'What other women?'

The vicar dispensed with the teacups and took a swig of the port from his bottle. 'Why those witches, of course,' he whispered in a low voice. 'Those devil women in tweed, the county's full of them.'

The vicar was surprised to find the captain a willing audience. Instead of calling for the landlord and having him thrown from the premises, this nice officer was ordering another bottle of the 'Portugal's' and asking him to continue. It was as if the floodgates of conversation had been lifted.

'Don't let the Victorian splendour of these mill towns fool you. The whole area is built on devilry and superstition. Scratch away the grime and what we're left with is the old religion. Witchcraft, my dear man!'

'Witchcraft?'

'Exactly!' The vicar snatched the glass of beer from the captain's hand and drank greedily from it. 'I have seen things in my parish that would turn your insides to water,' he said after burping loudly. 'Creatures that would terrify the Church of Rome. Think about it, fur-covered devils, black angels, and most horrible and fantastic of all...' He mouthed the word 'dragon' as though it were heresy to mention the creature's name in public.

The captain nudged his companion under the table, hardly believing what he'd heard.

'But you needn't take my word for it. Look at this.' The vicar dug deep into his leather bag and brought out a large brown envelope. He hesitated before giving it to the captain. 'I must warn you, what I am about to show you may test your faith as a Christian.'

Captain Dashing looked briefly inside the envelope and crossed his legs again; there was another crumpled photograph inside. The vicar grasped him by the sleeve. 'Be brave and resolute young soldier, take courage from our Lord.'

Private Oldfield gave a reassuring nod to the captain, who fearing the worst pulled the photograph out and placed it on the table with his eyes closed.

'Jesus H. Christ!' swore Private Oldfield, forgetting the company he was with and who he was supposed to be. The image displayed was of three of those dreadful women caught flying through the air and firing their shotguns. The vicar looked strangely pleased with his reaction.

'You took this picture?' the captain asked on opening his eyes.

'Almost a week ago, though it's not one of my best. Very difficult taking photographs in the dark.'

'It's unbelievable, these women are terrifying. Did you manage to photograph the dragon too?'

The vicar hugged himself with delight. 'I knew you would understand!' he cried. 'I could tell the moment I saw you. We are alike you and me, soldiers of a kind. But as for your question then no, you have only my word there that this creature exists.'

Captain Dashing tried to hide his disappointment. A photograph of the flying machine was just the evidence he needed.

'You could visit my parish though,' suggested the vicar mistaking the captain's expression as one of disbelief. 'It's the village of Sodden. There's a great hole in the middle of the street where the dragon crawled out of, and my church cracked and scorched with its steeple teetering over the edge. And what do my parishioners say, you may ask? Well, there's the treason, there's the devil's work. They say nothing. They walk about the village as though in a trance and blame everything on the council.'

'Surely not?'

'Oh yes, their minds are poisoned, and who is responsible? Miss Arabella Pike, that's who, the devil's disciple, a harpy in tweed!'

The captain could hardly believe his luck. He had stumbled across a walking crime report of information. 'You know this woman?' he asked.

'Know her? She's been the bane of my life, strutting through the village as though she owned the place, turning my parishioners against me. Why, she even tried to blow me up, and my church. My advice, if you see her, is to shoot on sight, but take care, she's not alone, there's a whole coven of them hereabouts.'

'Have you told anyone else about this?'

'Let us say I've tried, but there's no joy in being a voice in the wilderness, no joy at all. The Bishop thinks me mad, holds me responsible for the damage to his church. If it wasn't for this windfall, my days as vicar of the parish would be over.'

'You have money?'

The vicar shook the leather bag and rattled the gold coins. 'Oodles of the stuff, save it's not mine of course. How could it be, rich man, camel, eye of the needle and so forth. I intend to give it to the Bishop. I doubt it would cover the cost of repairs, but it's a start I suppose. On the other hand, there's much to be said for nipping off with the booty.'

Captain Dashing and Private Oldfield shook their heads.

'Absolutely,' said the vicar. 'That would be very wrong, forget I said it. Poor man, kingdom of heaven, open arms etcetera, etcetera.' His voice mumbled away into nothing until another idea struck him. 'On the other hand, you could be of some help. A friendly word in the Bishop's ear would go a long way. What about it?'

The captain shrugged his shoulders.

'I suppose you're right, no point in getting anyone else involved. Still, good of you to listen.'

The pork pie and port were beginning to take their effect. The vicar felt the need to close his mouth and swallow hard. 'So sorry,' he mumbled clutching the leather bag to his chest and stumbling to his feet. 'May have to say goodbye.' He lurched forward to shake the captain's hand but found himself kneeling on the carpet.

'Are you alright,' asked Private Oldfield, trying not to smile.

The vicar turned his head and tried to focus, but the kindly officer, and peculiar doctor of music were merging into one. 'Absolutely, never felt better.'

'We could hail you a cab; it might be safer than walking.'

The vicar screwed up his eyes, but the two faces refused to separate. 'No need, I could do with the exercise.' He pointed once more in the direction of Private Oldfield. 'Spitting image you are, quite frightening.' But before the doctor of music could protest, the vicar turned his attention to the far wall and shuffled on his knees across the carpet and out through the door.

'There's a stroke of luck,' whispered the captain. 'We've enough information now to make a difference. The stupid fool has even left us his photograph. It's our first piece of hard evidence. Here's to cheap port and loose tongues.' They tapped their glasses together and smiled. 'And may I say Private Oldfield, that your disguise was a triumph.'

'Are you sure? For a moment there I thought he'd seen right through me.'

'Nonsense, you've nothing to worry about. You saw his Venus with Arms, if that filthy swine can't tell the difference then who can?'

Chapter Four

The head keeper of Grubdale zoo arrived at work to find the place deserted. It was the last straw. Even the Indian Giraffe had disappeared.

'There aren't any giraffes in India,' a precocious little girl said while standing in front of the empty enclosure, licking a lollipop.

'Aye love, and now's there no bloody giraffes in Grubdale,' was the keeper's curt reply. The same could be said of all his exhibits, the last remaining few had vanished overnight. It was a pity the local press had got hold of the story. Losing one animal could be considered careless but losing an entire collection sold papers. The keeper ushered the little girl out of the zoo and had locked the gates behind her. He was never seen again.

'Out of all I think the zebras were the best,' mused the wyrm as she was hustled along the canal in the dark of night. 'Or maybe the penguins - chicken and fish in a feathery topping, very delicious.'

'I think we need to talk less and paddle more,' said Arabella, sitting astride the wyrm's head and holding up a lantern.

'There's still a long way to go before we reach Brideswell Locks.'

'But I'm bored, and when I'm bored, I think of food.'

This came as no surprise to Arabella. The enthusiasm with which the wyrm had taken to speaking with a northern accent, was only second to the way she'd treated the zoo as her personal larder. When asked by the professor why she hadn't touched the vegetables delivered to her each day, the question had been met with a look of haughty contempt. 'Because they give me gas,' she had said. 'And when I get gas I make flames. It's not something my public wish to see, a 'giraffe' burning at both ends.'

The ancient texts had hinted at the considerable intelligence of the great wyrms, but this capacity for rational argument had surprised even the professor. He was at a loss for a reply, and from that day forward had decided to remove Her Majesty from the zoo to a more appropriate hiding place, and not before time. The news in the local press was that Grubdale was under siege from all the 'escaped' animals. With the banner headline 'IT'S A JUNGLE OUT THERE,' the front page of the Grubdale Clarion described the unfortunate experiences of one Reverend Cross while returning home from late night communion. Not only had he been set upon by a group of vicious penguins, but after fleeing up a narrow side street, had trodden on the tail of a large Bengal tiger. The accompanying photograph of a bruised and battered vicar, looking pitifully at the camera lens while trying to hold up his trousers was proof enough; the streets were alive with exotic beasts. Even a group of nuns had been pounced upon by an old baboon smelling of port and pork pie, before managing to frighten it away with their boots and fists. Now every Tom, Dick or Harry with a gun was on the rampage, shooting at anything that moved or made a noise in the shadows. It was a bad night to be out on the streets.

'I don't see why I can't fly to this Brideswell place,' the wyrm complained. 'It would take less time.'

Arabella swung the lantern to each side, trying to get her bearings. 'The professor insisted,' she said. 'No flying unless absolutely necessary. His orders were most specific; we must make our way along the canal as quiet as possible and wait for him at Brideswell Locks.'

'I suppose there I can shake off this blasted collar. It's awkward pretending to be a barge with my head as a smokestack.'

It had been one of the professor's better ideas, to disguise the wyrm as a canal boat. The waterways passed close by to the zoo and all that was required were a few minutes slithering through the back fields to a quiet stretch of the Grubdale canal. There amongst the reeds had lain an old barge with a note attached from the professor.

'It seems you're to burn the bottom out,' Arabella read as she stood on the bank. 'I presume by that he means the boat. It's so that you can slip inside and put your head through the hole like a chimney. How ingenious.'

The wyrm was of a different opinion. 'It looks a tight fit to me,' she said. 'Do you think the man has thought this through?'

'I expect so. We've all seen you make a pig of yourself. I bet that's the biggest boat he could find.'

'It's a ridiculous idea; nothing less than an insult. He's making me wear an iron skirt.'

'Oh do stop complaining and hurry up, we've a long way to travel yet.'

'Not even my colour. Look at it, it's filthy.'

The wyrm continued to complain even as she dived underwater, her moaning and grumbling bubbling up to the surface like little pockets of gas. But it was a skirt nonetheless, and the wyrm was nothing if not fashionable. 'How do I look?' she asked after pushing her head through the roof.

'Like a 'Coal Scuttle.'

'What?'

'It's the name of the barge. It's painted on the side.'

'The professor's idea of a joke I suppose; I would have thought a little more respect was in order, considering my position. He should have found one with a prettier name.'

And so they had continued, the wyrm making heavy weather of wading through the silt, and with Arabella holding up the lantern and calling out directions. After an hour or more of slow progress, the lock gates came into view.

'You can stop paddling now, Your Majesty,' Arabella whispered. 'I'm sure that's Brideswell ahead.'

The wyrm let out a sigh of relief. 'And not soon enough, I've cramp in my toes.'

They drifted forward until the bow of the barge bumped into the side of the bank. Arabella took hold of the rope and jumped ashore. 'Try and keep the boat still,' she said tying the rope to an iron ring. 'We don't want your stern to swing around.'

'Well really! Could anyone be more personal?'

After securing the barge to the canal bank, Arabella stepped back on board and turned the handle of the galley door.

'And where do you think you're going?' the wyrm asked.

'I'm going to bed. I doubt the Professor will arrive before morning.'

'Not down there you're not. It's a tight squeeze as it is.' There was the tiniest hint of triumph in the wyrm's voice.

Arabella opened the door and stared at a wall of scales. It was useless to argue. The wyrm had expanded to fill every inch of the barge. 'I told you so, not something the professor had thought of, is it? I suggest you sleep outside.'

Arabella buttoned her coat to the top and sat down on the open deck. 'Sweet dreams,' whispered the wyrm as she rested her head on the roof. 'Pleasant dreams yourself,' snapped Arabella, thinking entirely the opposite.

The first trills of the dawn chorus whistled through the trees, and Arabella awoke to find she was up to her waist in the cold waters of the canal.

'Good morning Miss Pike,' greeted a smiling Professor Broadbent from the safety of the bank. 'You look a little damp.'

Arabella waded across and grasped his outstretched hand. 'I would appreciate it if you didn't state the obvious,' she said through chattering teeth as she was pulled up the bank. 'I'm soaked to the skin.'

'So I see,' the professor said, looking at the half sunken barge with disappointment. He pushed the side with his foot, but the barge refused to move. 'It would appear Her Majesty has shed her disguise. Really, Miss Pike, this is most unfortunate. I've important questions I need to ask.'

'Most unfortunate? I could think of a better description. How about selfish or just plain bloody-minded? Look at me, my clothes are ruined.' Arabella was not in the best of humour. She would have laughed in her younger days, but now of a certain age, waking up in a pair of cold, wet underwear with pondweed in her stockings was too much.

'Isn't there a spell you could use? I'm sure it's not the end of the world.'

'There you go again,' Arabella fumed, 'stating the damned obvious. Is that all it takes to become a professor? I tell you, I'm having second thoughts about this mission. Her Majesty has done nothing but eat and complain. It's like living with Rowena.' She twirled her index finger in a circle and pointed at her legs, casting the 'Warm Wind of Flagellum' all up her front and causing her cheeks to flush.

'Better now?' asked the professor. 'Good, then take a look at this.' He threw her a rolled up copy of the Bangor Herald. 'Read the first page,' he said. 'It should interest you.'

Arabella shook the newspaper flat as though it were a linen shirt left outside in a frost. The banner headline read 'THE RED DRAGON OF WALES.' She looked over the top at the professor, her eyes wide with astonishment.

'Read on,' the professor said. 'It gets better.'

The article carried a series of cave paintings each depicting the unmistakable image of a dragon jumping through a flaming hoop. They'd been discovered on the walls of a cave near a Welsh village whose name covered at least three columns in its spelling.

'Do the flames remind you of anything?' asked the professor.

'A gateway?'

'Precisely, Miss Pike, you state the obvious. You have the makings of a professor after all. Look at the dragon, not at all like Her Majesty is it? I took the trouble of telephoning the editor; the drawings were painted in red ochre.'

'Which means?'

'Oh come on Miss Pike. We have all read the old texts. These are paintings of an Emperor Wyrm. To think how stupid we have been, stumbling about in the dark in search of clues, and all the time the biggest clue of all was flying on

71

every flag west of Offa's Dike. The Red Dragon, Miss Pike – the emblem of Wales. If it were ever possible to meet the Stone Age man responsible then I swear I would hug him. I'm so happy. Don't you see how close we are, two wyrms for the price of one!'

'Two Great Wyrms?'

'Look closely at the pictures, tell me what you see?'

'A badly drawn wyrm with eight legs?'

'Precisely, you have it in one. I can't believe our good luck. See, these are the original photographs.' The professor handed Arabella a large envelope. 'There are two wyrms depicted.'

Arabella opened the envelope and examined the prints. 'I can only see one,' she said.

'Look again at that squiggly bit in the background. It's as plain as the nose on your face. It's another head.'

Professor Broadbent stood patiently by, rocking to and fro on his heels and jingling the change in his pocket as Arabella held the photographs up to the morning light. He was the very picture of smugness, like a cat that had got the cream. 'How does the popular saying go?' he said. 'You wait all day for one bus, then all three come along at the same time.'

Arabella had heard of something similar. 'I hate to be a fly in the custard,' she said, 'but shouldn't we tread cautiously? After all, we don't want to count wyrms until the eggs are hatched.'

The professor stopped rattling his change and looked puzzled at Arabella. 'What was that you said?' he asked, smiling. 'I swear you're talking in riddles, simple sentences will suffice.'

Arabella pointed at a series of scribbles in the bottom corner of one of the photographs. There was a heart with an arrow through it. 'Are you sure these drawings are genuine?

What about the writing, UGG LUBS HUGGA-BUGGA. What can that mean?'

'Quite simply Miss Pike, that a very long time ago someone called UGG loved someone called HUGGA-BUGGA.'

'Are you saying that Stone Age man could write?'

'Why not, who knows what influence these wyrms had on our past. It seems only a small step from producing paintings like these to the occasional spelling mistake.'

Arabella shook her head. There was little difference between the cave paintings and Rowena's unfortunate photograph of the Loch Ness Monster. They were most likely fakes, and she lost no time in pointing this out to Professor Broadbent.

'At the end of the day, Miss Pike, that's why I am a professor and you're not. You have overlooked the most important detail. Only someone who has seen a wyrm or a wyrmhole could have painted something like this, and that's why I must speak with Her Majesty. Her information is invaluable.'

As if on cue the brambles beside the towpath pushed apart, and the head of Her Majesty poked through, chewing what looked suspiciously like a cow's hoof. 'I refuse to climb back into that contraption!' she said indicating the barge with her head. 'I am a queen and as a queen I think little of being daubed with yellow paint and squeezed into a 'Coal Scuttle.' There shall be no more disguises. It is my last word on the matter.'

Professor Broadbent bowed. 'Your Majesty, I must apologise. These were necessary precautions, for your safety if nothing else.'

The wyrm leant close to the professor and raised one of her claws. With a snap like the breaking of a chicken bone, five razor-sharp talons shot out. She tapped the professor under the jaw. 'Don't you think I'm well able to take care of myself?' she mewed.

'Of course you are, but Grubdale is a primitive town, full of cruel, little people.'

The wyrm scratched the professor's chin gently. 'And that should be a problem for me?'

Professor Broadbent tried a different approach. 'It's not a respectable place; no queen should be seen there.'

Arabella raised her eyes. What a stupid thing to say, she thought. For all her faults, the wyrm would hardly be swayed by such a lame remark, yet Her Majesty retracted her talons and studied the professor carefully. 'And that would be wrong?' she asked.

'Very wrong, Your Majesty. For royalty to be seen on those streets would be like social suicide, the very equivalent of dressing up in one's finery and treading in something unpleasant.'

'How unpleasant?'

'The very worst, like the bottom of the lion's cage after the liver and onions.'

The wyrm shrugged her shoulders. She had to concede that the professor had a point.

'If it would please Your Majesty,' the professor continued. 'I could arrange transport to more suitable quarters. What I have in mind would be perfect. There would be no question of a disguise.'

'I expect nothing less than a palace.'

'It will be all of that if not in name. There will be people to look after your every want. Important personages will travel the length and breadth of the country just to catch a glimpse of your beauty. They would pay money for the privilege.'

The wyrm thought awhile on what Professor Broadbent had said, chewing on the more resilient morsels of breakfast. 'And is that not common?'

'Not at all, Your Majesty.'

'Then I accept, but on one account, no vegetables or greenery of any kind.'

'Definitely no vegetables,' Arabella interrupted.

'And where is this palace?'

The professor looked at Arabella; he could hardly say a circus. 'In North Wales, a beautiful country of lakes, mountains and endless sheep…'

'Not to mention dragons,' Arabella added before being kicked hard on the shin by the professor. The wyrm raised herself to her full height, her nostrils flaring as if to deliver a scythe of flame. She had begun to get used to the prospect of being the centre of attention. One of the weaknesses of being as old as coal was a streak of selfishness the width of Alaska. 'You mean I am not alone?' she said.

'To be entirely honest, Your Majesty, we're not sure. What Miss Pike was referring to, so rudely,' - there was a snort from Arabella – 'are a collection of cave drawings. Perhaps you could take a look at these and give us your opinion?' The professor snatched the prints from Arabella and placed them down on the ground in front of the wyrm. Her Majesty lowered her head over the brambles until her nose was inches away then, looking quickly at the professor from out of the corner of her eye, moved even closer.

'I can't make out a thing,' she dismissed, not wanting to admit to failing eyesight. 'The images are too small.' She felt a nudge on her snout as someone held a large magnifying glass in front.

'Perhaps this would be of help?' suggested the professor. 'Now tell me, what can you see?'

'A dirty thumbnail,' the wyrm answered.

'Can't you make out the image of an Emperor? I thought it was obvious.'

The wyrm's eyes locked with those of the professor. 'Here, give me that thing,' she snapped, and screwing the magnifying glass into one of her eye sockets, she proceeded to scan the photographs with a sense of urgency. It was clear to Arabella that the wyrm was unhappy. Perhaps it was feminine intuition or maybe the way the creature flicked the photographs into the canal after looking at each one.

'Well?' asked the professor trying to fish out the photographs from the water. 'Any comments?'

Her Majesty removed the magnifying glass and threw it on the ground in disgust. 'Only one,' she said. 'Who's the floozy in the background, that's what I want to know.'

Professor Broadbent clapped his hands. 'I was right!' he shouted. 'You see Miss Pike, there are two dragons!'

'Wyrms, Professor Broadbent! We are Wyrms! And now I have a favour to ask. How do I get to this cave?' There was a tone in her voice that indicated any refusal would be met with a sharp blast of hot air.

'Of course Your Majesty, it would be my pleasure. But may I ask why?'

'No, you may not!' said the wyrm. There was a moment's unease before the wyrm lowered her voice. 'It is a personal matter, not something a gentleman should ask. We must go to this place of drawings at once. Who knows what the fool's been up to?'

'The fool? Are you saying you recognise a dragon in the picture?'

76

The professor's question was met with an icy silence, and it was Arabella's turn to kick someone on the shin. 'Can't you see she's upset,' she whispered. The professor hopped on one foot and cursed under his breath. But not even this could spoil his excitement. The wyrm was proving more useful than he could have imagined. She would be their bloodhound, sniffing out her fellow creatures from the soil. And timely too, for on a distant planet a little to the left and slightly down from the buckle on Orion's belt, Bethesda Chubb was beginning to talk.

The Sisterhood would have been delighted their hot-headed companion was still alive. Bethesda, on the other hand, was not. She'd woken up with a splitting headache, lips like two bananas, and an eye that refused to open. It was as if she'd spent the night on the tequila slammers and picked a fight with a bear. She lay on her back and tried to remember what had happened, or if she was still in a dream. One thing was certain, Bethesda Chubb was back at home. There were two orange moons in the sky, fell wolves were howling in the distance and the air rich with the familiar scent of crushed oilweed. There were more obvious clues. She was bound with chains, locked inside a cage, and dragged slowly uphill on top of a large cart; not the sort of treatment a young lady would expect in Derbyshire, except on her wedding day.

For the first moment in her life, Bethesda Chubb was scared. This was no group of policemen escorting her back to a warm cell and a bowl of soup, but a pack of snarling rat-things - Rattus erectus, or whatever Professor Broadbent had called them. She'd been kidnapped by the enemy. As an act of defiance, or else from pure fear, Bethesda kicked out at the iron bars and screamed.

'Hey, you there!' shouted a scruffily dressed human walking beside the cart. 'Anymore of that noise and I'll rip out your tongue!' It was a surprising threat to make from someone escorting a prisoner for interrogation. The man hit one of the rat-things around the head for the sheer hell of it, and pushed his way to the front of the procession. 'She's playing up that one,' he said to the driver of the cart. 'I had to threaten her.'

'That was brave,' said the man, cracking his whip over the backs of the buffagrunts as they struggled to pull the cart along the forest path. 'Seeing as she's all tied up. Who is she anyway?'

'What is she? you mean. She's a witch.'

The driver smiled and drew his finger across his throat. 'Then it's the chop for her, I shouldn't wonder. Our Mr Spleen has a thing about witches.'

The man looked behind at the cage. 'Aye,' he said. 'And I wish he'd have a thing or two about rats as well. They seem a little skittish tonight.'

The rat-things were more than skittish. True to form they were terrified. The forest was all shadows and whispers, and it hadn't escaped their attention that the path was scattered with tell-tale signs of a Jellico on the prowl. It was bandit country too. While the sorcerer had few enemies, those that had survived had peculiar habits, like painting their faces black, jumping out from the darkness and generally separating people limb from limb. It paid to be safe, so the rat-things had their pistols cocked, and were almost walking backwards in their attempt to screen the cart.

'What's happened to the boss?' asked the driver, unnerved by the various animal noises in the forest. 'They're terrified of him.'

By 'him', the driver meant Vermyn Stench, the sorcerer's head of secret police, a terrible rat beast – half man, half rat and all bad. It was Stench who'd captured Miss Chubb, and it was Stench who'd taken great pains to ensure poor Bethesda was tied up securely and locked in a cage.

The prisoner's escort shrugged his shoulders. 'I'm not sure where he is. Probably back in Spleen's laboratory getting patched up. He looked a little torn around the edges, last I saw of him.'

'Not many edges by all account. You've heard about his missing arm? Rumour is he gnawed it off as a mark of obedience.'

'Is that what they say? I heard it was his claw, and that he'd caught it in a trap when pinching the cheese.'

The two men laughed as they guided the cart along the steep track, oblivious to the crack of a musket in the distance, as the first bullet struck home. A rat-thing fell over.

'Get up you lazy git!' shouted the scruffily dressed man. He kicked the body as he walked past, only for it to roll over and reveal a small hole in the creature's chest that was leaking goo and bubbles. A second bullet whizzed past and clipped a large splinter of wood off the side of the cart.

'Who did that?' shouted the man, turning on the rat-things huddled in a group behind. 'Come on, own up!' The tall rodents chattered nervously to each other and hid their weapons behind their backs. The man lifted the largest by the scruff of its neck and shook it violently. 'Your nothing but useless, how many times do we tell you - keep your fingers off those triggers.'

The third bullet struck the unfortunate rodent through its head, its two eyes turned backwards as though jerked by a string.

'Ambush!' shouted the man, and flung the body aside. 'Take cover!' He pulled a large flintlock pistol from his belt and fired it into the distance, causing a large branch to crack and fall to the floor. The rat-things looked at each other then fired off a volley of shots. There was a sudden explosion and a tower of flame tore its way up through the forest, high into the night sky. The rat-creatures' mouths fell open, their frightened faces outlined in the harsh light. Shadows that went 'boom' in the night could mean only one thing – Raggedies!

Panic spread through the small group of rat soldiers as they struggled to re-load their pistols, dropping ramrods and spilling gunpowder on the ground as though it was confetti. Raggedies hated rats and weren't too fond of humans neither, they hated just about anything that trespassed through their forest. They were tall, spindly creatures all wrapped in rags and dipped in oil, and had a nasty habit of exploding when angry. Some thought them ghosts, the spirits of long dead kings, whilst others were not so generous.

The man clambered aboard the cart and shouted at the driver to make the beasts go faster. The buffagrunts pulled and strained at their ropes, but were beasts of burden, not used to cantering down a race track and jumping over hedges. 'Just my luck,' he moaned, pulling out a blunderbuss from a side pannier and climbing on top of the cage. 'Keep this wreck steady while I try a shot.'

'Make sure you don't miss!' shouted the driver.

The man lay down on the roof of the cage and pulled himself along to the rear, making sure not to spill the bent nails and washers rattling around in his blunderbuss. Someone screamed, and a tattered figure leapt from nowhere, somersaulting in the sky to land amongst a group of rat-things.

It spun around in a circle as an arc of flame sliced through fur and bone.

'Got you!' shouted the man and fired his blunderbuss at the whirling raggedy. He missed. The spectral figure had leapt back into the darkness, and the man's shot merely added to the carnage below. 'And what are you staring at?' he asked as the rat-things glared at him suspiciously. 'It's not my fault these gas-bags just disappear.' He threw the blunderbuss to the ground and pulled out a second pistol from his belt. Another scream split the air as the raggedy leapt past, and the rat's fired off a second volley splintering the wood of the cage roof around the man's head.

'Where did it go?' the driver shouted, urging the buffagrunts forward.

'How the hell do I know, and keep your eyes on the road!'

A large stone on the track caused the cart to jump and the man on the roof was thrown over on his back. He swore as he looked up at the legs of the tattered figure standing over him, and the last thought that went through his mind as he pulled the trigger of his pistol was 'Oooops!' There was a loud explosion as both he and the raggedy disappeared in a burst of flame, and to the dismay of the rats as they covered up their ears from the noise, the buffagrunts decided to break into a gallop.

'Come on you lot,' cried the driver as he did his best to steer the smouldering cart. 'Keep up if you can!' The rat-things needed no encouragement. They sprinted off after the cart and scrambled aboard, hanging from the bars of the cage for dear life. There was a crack of a musket being fired, and the final victim fell to the floor with a neat hole in the back of its skull. Another raggedy stepped out of the trees into the middle of the track and lowered its long-barrelled weapon and watched as the cart sped off into the distance. Here was news to tell and a mystery to be solved, one of the Sisterhood had been captured by the enemy.

Chapter Five

Bethesda wished she was like Arabella – fat; a healthy state of plumpness to cushion her against the bumps and jerks of the cart as it trundled along the pitted tracks of the road. A lot of things had changed in the country since she'd been away, and adequate suspension was one. She'd been bounced and thrown around the cage like dice in a cup, and the chains that bound her body were a poor substitute for a well-upholstered figure. To her relief the cart had come to a sudden stop, and from the distant noise of waves crashing against rocks, and the pecking of a large gull that had decided to hitch a ride on top of her head, Bethesda Chubb realised she was somewhere near the sea. She twisted herself around on the bottom of the cage and tried to look up through the bars. All she could make out was a large yellow beak and the upside-down face of an inquisitive bird staring back.

'Clear off!' she hissed as she shook her head, but the seagull gave her nose an affectionate tweak and hung on to her hair even tighter. It was as though she had been adopted by the bird. Three times during their journey it had flown off into the distance only to return some minutes later and regurgitate fish paste all down her shoulder. It was either very motherly or a terrible traveller.

The driver pulled the cart to a stop outside the gates of a gigantic wall and engaged in conversation with a group of soldiers obviously interested in his prisoner.

'A witch you say,' said the sergeant-at-arms. 'So this is what the Master's been afraid of.' He walked to the back of the cart and rattled the bars of the cage with his halberd. 'She doesn't look dangerous to me.'

The driver jumped down from his seat and stood by the sergeant's side. 'That may be so,' he said. 'But looks aren't everything. Who knows what'll happen if those chains fall off.'

'Nothing that a jab of steel won't cure. Why, look at this,' the sergeant said as another of the soldiers poked at the bird on Bethesda's head with a stick. 'She's sprouted a hat.

'What's the matter sweetheart, trying to look your best for the Master? It won't do much good, not where you're going.'

The seagull hated sticks even more than she hated her noisy neighbours, squawking all day and turning her cliff to a fish-reeking mire. Sticks were the tools of the collector; red-faced climbers who dangled from ropes and knocked you off your roost with a well-aimed prod. She snapped with her beak at the offending piece of wood, her mind full of the thoughts of precious eggs stuffed into trouser pockets and their contents being blown away at the end of a straw.

'I'd take that hat back to the shops if I were you,' laughed the soldier, fending off the seagull with the occasional swipe. 'It's turned vicious.'

The driver tapped him on the shoulder. 'No, wait, listen to this,' he guffawed, 'I've got a better one. It's not an 'at but one of those 'familiars''.

It had been meant as a joke, and not a good one at that, but the effect was far from hilarious. The soldier withdrew his stick and took a few steps away from the cage. 'I hadn't thought of that,' he said wiping the palm of his hand on his trousers, and neither had the driver until then. A common or garden witch was one thing, mixing up potions and casting the odd small spell or two, but witches with familiars were a different barrel of fish heads altogether. Those sorts of women spelt trouble. 'Ere, you don't think she's one of the Sisterhood?' he asked the driver, nervously. 'They can turn nasty, so I've been told.'

'I dunno, but the Master seems to want her pretty bad, and I'm not thinking cotton sheets, if you get my meaning.'

The soldier shuddered at the thought and dropped his stick. If the rumours were true then he'd just spent the last few minutes prodding at someone who, by the slightest snap of her fingers, could turn his whole body to ice, and chisel off the winter baubles as an encore.

'You could 'ave told us,' whispered the sergeant-at-arms, edging sideways to the front of the cart. 'The sooner we get this woman inside and off our hands the better.'

'I'm right behind you there,' whispered the driver from right behind him, and together the two climbed on the driving board and waited for the sentries on top of the castle walls to wake up and realise there was someone outside wanting to come in.

'And about bleedin' time too!' shouted the driver, hearing the noise of posteriors being kicked and levers being pulled. 'We've an urgent delivery for the Master!'

There was the rattle and clank of chains being hauled over giant cogs, and slowly the two enormous steel doors that led into the castle grounds swung apart. The driver cracked his whip over the top of the buffagrunt's heads. 'Come on my beauties, don't give up on me now,' he said. The animals strained and pulled, and pulled and strained, but were good for nothing but the butcher and a one-way recipe for beef curry.

The sergeant snatched the whip away and hit the beasts sharply on their rumps. 'Don't molly-coddle the buggers, give it to 'em 'ard!' he shouted. 'I want to be shot of that woman before she 'as it in for me!'

The cart lurched forward sending Bethesda rolling to the back of the cage, and the seagull flying off for yet another fish supper.

'See, all that's needed is a strong arm.'

The driver snatched the whip back and shook the reins in disgust. He guided the cart between the narrow opening of the steel doors and through into the main square, with what remained of his escort of rat-things following behind. He stood up from his seat and shouted to what appeared to be an officer in charge, a large bulbous man astride a most unfortunate pony.

'Where do you want us to park? We've a dangerous prisoner tied up in the back.'

The officer rode up to the cart and took a quick peek inside the cage, before steering his pony quickly around.

'Take yourselves off to the castle steps and be quick about it. Stench is waiting for you and he's not too happy about it.'

Bethesda shivered at the mention of the creature's name. Whatever happens, she thought, I must be brave, for the sake of the Sisterhood. But her imagination was beginning to get the better of her, and from the look of the castle as it appeared out of the darkness, she was in for serious trouble. It was a question of numbers, or towers to be precise. Mad Kings had a weakness for them. Less than three and the worst you could

86

expect was a saucy wink and a chase around the royal bedchamber. More than ten and they'd use gadgets. Bethesda gulped; she'd never seen a building so rich with towers before. It was like a gigantic bundle of asparagus, closely packed and simmering in the mist. Whoever lived here must be a very bad boy indeed.

Vermyn Stench stood at the bottom of the steps, his body swathed from head to toe in bandages and with his tail thumping angrily on the cobblestones. He was in a terrible humour and feeling a little thin on the inside. It was one of the downsides of being indestructible. For the last two hours he'd been laid out on a slab having his wings removed. He'd watched significant parts of his innards being washed down the sink as the medics snipped away with their scissors, chasing a multitude of shotgun pellets all around his body. He leant on his claw-tipped cane and stretched the tired muscles in his back. Any more battles like the last and he'd have to stuff the empty spaces with straw just to stand up.

There was the noise of cattle straining at the yoke. Stench narrowed his eyes to see through the gap in his bandages. So, his prisoner had arrived at last, he thought. How unlucky for her. He stepped in front of the cart and held out his claw to stop.

'Sorry to be late,' the driver said, pulling the exhausted buffagrunts to a halt. 'But we bumped into a group of raggedies on the way.'

Stench dismissed the excuse with a snort. They'd arrived, that was all he wanted to know. He walked slowly around to the side of the cage and peered at the chained figure in the shadows.

'Charming,' the driver whispered to the sergeant-at-arms. 'I tell you something, mate. If we 'ad snouts and tails it'd be a different story. We'd be a few coins richer and full of cheese by now. Smarmy little soldier rats are all over 'im. I'd some pet mice once. You'd be surprised what they get up to.'

'You don't have to tell me - the wife's from down south.'

This small point was lost on the driver. He shook his head, fumbled about in his top pocket for a smoke, and thanked the heavens he was a single man. Not that he was a stranger to women, just that he'd never met one who liked to spin around in a wire wheel or chew his mattress to pulp. He pondered the matter some more till a brisk fanfare of trumpets caused everyone to drop what they were doing and stand smartly to attention.

'Blimey, we're honoured today,' said the sergeant. 'The Master himself is coming out.'

'Let's hope he keeps his mask on. I've caught sight of 'is face before and it'd turn your guts to water. He might be all powerful, but he's no charmer. Front of the queue for the ugly stick was our Mr Spleen.'

Bethesda, startled at the mention of the sorcerer's name, realised she'd lost. She'd been wrapped up and delivered to Spleen's doorstep as easy as a pint of milk. There would be no last-minute rescue, no brave speech from the gallows. She would be made to talk and then what? Bethesda tried to blank the image from her mind. Why had she thought of a bottle of milk? All she could picture now was her brain being pecked at like sparrows after the cream.

Bethesda struggled to her feet and leant heavily against the bars, her mind racing with thoughts of what to do next. Escape was impossible, and it would only be a matter of time before she gave in to the horrors of the laboratory. What was important was that the Big Secret remained safe. Spleen and his followers must never know about the prince. She fought back tears as she realised what she must do.

'Hey, Nephertiti!' Bethesda shouted, nervously. 'Yes, you in the bandages! What's the matter? Fell into a patch of nettles?'

Stench stood with his back to Bethesda, ignoring her catcalls.

'Oy, I'm talking to you, you overgrown owl pellet!' she cried. 'Come over here and finish what you started!'

Bethesda tried to spit but could only manage a wet dribble down her chin, her mouth too dry from fear. 'Mother's boy! Stinkwort! Lick-spittle! Coward…'

Stench turned to face her, his eyes red with rage. He thought little of the insults, but some of the soldier rats were laughing behind their claws.

Bethesda resumed her attack. 'You don't scare me Mr Vermyn Stench' she hissed. 'Standing there in all your puff and padding. Call yourself a man - I've kicked the dentures from bigger idiots than you.'

Stench's eyes narrowed. He opened his mouth to snarl, causing a tear to appear in the strips of muslin wrapped around his head. Bethesda saw his weakness and struck home.

'They're laughing at you Mr Stench,' she continued.

'Speak for yourself,' whispered the driver trying to slide off the cart while no one was looking.

'Yeah, leave me out of this an' all,' added the guard following close behind. 'What's she trying to do – start a bleedin' war?'

'They might be frightened of you,' Bethesda cried. 'But there's no respect. Listen…'

As if on cue a soldier rat coughed to stop himself from giggling and was immediately kicked in the shins by his nervous comrades.

'Even your soldiers think you're a joke. The great Vermyn Stench, the hero of the hour. Chased away by a small, pink poodle.'

Stench's shoulders shook with rage.

Bethesda continued her attack. 'Why, you've not told them, have you?' she said, then repeated the words 'small,' 'pink' and 'poodle' so that everyone could hear.

Stench could contain himself no longer. He raised his claw-topped cane and brought it down hard on the cobblestones of the courtyard, causing a shower of sparks to settle at his feet. At once there was a rush of air, expanding and throwing everyone aside, then a terrible explosion of sound that set the windows of the castle rattling in their frames. The bars of the cage fell apart, and before Bethesda had a chance to ready herself for the shock, her body flew upwards through the shattered roof and stayed there, spinning in the air.

An ornate, carved palanquin appeared at the top of the steps. 'NO!' shouted a voice from behind the curtains. 'LEAVE HER TO ME!'

Stench let go of his cane and Bethesda fell down hard at his feet, a bruised and winded bundle of rags, furious at being alive. Bethesda had failed the Sisterhood. Now there would be nothing but pain and the certainty of her voice screaming out secrets one by one.

Stench kept his head lowered as the palanquin was carried slowly down the steps, eight soldiers of the Imperial Legion making hard work of supporting its weight on their shoulders.

'I told you not to harm the woman,' the voice said. 'We will talk of this later.'

Stench growled quietly to himself. The sorcerer's talks were legendary, and had little to do with tea and ginger biscuits.

The soldiers lowered the palanquin to the floor, straining their backs and popping a few vertebrae in the process.

'Welcome to Castle Arachnid,' said the voice. Bethesda opened her eyes and saw a haze of yellow silk, with strange designs embroidered in silver and gold swirling on the surface. The sorcerer disliked being seen in public and had taken to hiding behind curtains whenever possible.

'I had hoped your arrival would have been more civilised. But what can I do? Commander Stench is an excellent policeman, but knows little of the rules of our game. I blame his parents, except he has none, I made him myself. Still, there's no reason we can't be civil to one another. Here, take my hand.'

Something like a hand appeared from behind the curtains and brushed against Bethesda's cheek leaving a red welt where it touched the skin. Bethesda cried out in pain and rolled away.

'That's nothing to what I have in store for you inside,' said the voice, softly.

Bethesda swore in her best gutter-dialogue. 'Lay a hand on me,' she said, 'and you'll be laughing on the other side of your face!'

The curtains opened. 'You mean like this?' asked the voice, and Bethesda saw the terrible Tarantulus Spleen for the first time and screamed. So did the driver.

'Take her to the laboratory,' the voice ordered. 'I'll deal with her after breakfast.' At the mention of 'breakfast' a few poor unfortunates in the dungeon started to groan and cry out for mercy. Spleen had simple tastes. He liked his steaks rare and talkative in the morning.

Serrin Gutterprod was a nervous man; two years as chief torturer and 'Wielder of the Big Syringe' had made him so, and if there was one lesson he'd learnt while heating irons and turning screws it was this – only a fool would get on the wrong side of Spleen. Serrin's hands shook as he tried to wash the ink off his fingers. He'd never written so many words in one sitting. There were pages of the morning's confessional all over the floor.

'You appear to have started without me.'

Serrin dropped the soap in surprise. Tarantulus Spleen had a habit of creeping up unawares.

'It's the prisoner Sire, she won't shut up. All I did was wheel a trolley of glassware out of the drying oven, and she took one look at it and started to blab.'

Serrin averted his eyes from the reflection in the washroom mirror. Tarantulus Spleen was ugly enough the right way around without having to look at him back to front. 'I've not seen anything like it. One glance at a funnel and stopcock, and the woman's giving me her life story. It's been impossible to write it all down.'

'I don't want her biography, Mr Gutterprod. I want to know what the sisterhood are doing.' 'Oh, it'll be ages before I find out that,' Serrin said, as he bent down to pick up the soap. 'My nib broke during her teenage years, and that was half an hour ago at least. Apparently, her life went downhill the day she felt something strange in a grocery queue. She's been 'off' men ever since.'

Serrin threw the soap back in the basin, but couldn't help a sharp intake of breath as he saw Spleen's face in the mirror, a masked face covered in yellow leather like a skull. Spleen said nothing, but held Serrin's gaze for a few moments before blinking. The torturer flinched a second time.

'You have an expressive face Mr Gutterprod, not a virtue in your job, I think.'

Serrin laughed nervously and wiped his hands on the side of his lab-coat. 'We should go in,' he said, trying to change the conversation. Spleen nodded his head and followed the man out of the washroom, his limbs hardly seeming to move beneath the thick folds of his robe, but with the sound of more than one pair of feet tapping on floor. Serrin felt his stomach grow cold. He tried not to think what moved beneath the gold embroidery. There were rumours, of course, but nothing any sane man would consider possible.

'The prisoner is over here,' Serrin said, pointing at Bethesda.

Poor Bethesda. She was suspended from the ceiling by chains, and recounting as she span slowly around, the glorious days when fruit was 10 shellocks a pound and the village band played music you could dance to. Tarantulus Spleen walked across the room and stood close by her, seemingly interested in this stream of banal memories spouting forth. He raised a yellow-gloved hand and clicked his fingers.

'Name?' he asked.

'Chubb, Bethesda,' answered Serrin referring to his notes.

Without warning Spleen grasped Bethesda by the hair and pulled her face to his. 'I am not a fool Miss Chubb,' he whispered into her ear. 'And neither, I think, are you. Kindly stop this playacting. You're convincing no one but Mr Gutterprod, and even he's tired of writing what you say. You will address yourself to my questions, and these alone. That way we both finish before supper, what? Now answer me this, are you acquainted with an organisation known as the Sisterhood?'

Bethesda refused to speak, her fear replaced with seething rage.

'A simple 'yes' will suffice.'

Bethesda remained silent. Spleen moved her head up and down as though Bethesda was nothing but a ventriloquist's doll.

'Take that as a positive, Mr Gutterprod.'

Serrin nodded, and after looking for a new pen, scribbled something down on a sheet of parchment. Tarantulus waited until he'd finished, then asked another question.

'You are a member of this organisation. Am I correct?'

Bethesda stared at Spleen's masked face and gauged the distance between her teeth and his throat. It would require all her powers of concentration, and the last ounce of her strength. She closed her eyes and focussed her mind then, with a blinding flash of light, transformed her appearance to a rabid wolf and lunged at the Sorcerer. Spleen let go of her head and stepped back out of harm's way, smiling at the ridiculous image of a middle-aged woman with a dog's head snap and snarl, and spin around like a puppet.

'Let's dispense with these cheap tricks, Miss Chubb,' he said. 'You'll only make yourself dizzy.'

Bethesda returned to her normal shape and hung there, panting and wheezing, her energy spent.

'You disappoint me, Miss Chubb. I expected a more worthy opponent. I'll ask you again, are you a member of the Sisterhood?'

Bethesda slowly raised her head and shook the sweat from her eyes. It was pointless to deny the fact. With a note of defiance in her voice she shouted that she was, and proud to be considered the same.

'Then you are guilty of treason, Miss Chubb, and there can be only one outcome. You will be taken from here tomorrow to a place of execution and broken on the wheel until dead.'

Serrin shuddered, it was a most horrible way to die.

'I am however, a reasonable man…' There was a noticeable silence as Serrin raised his pen from the parchment in disbelief.

'I could always reconsider – let you off for good behaviour. All I need are facts, Miss Chubb. Facts are more valuable than gold. In your case, doubly so. This Big Secret of yours, what does it mean?'

Bethesda's closed her eyes and tried to fight back the tears. Spleen knew more than she'd thought.

'No matter,' said Spleen. 'There are clues. Stench is convinced your plans involve the old religion, the worship of the Great Wyrms. How sad, I would hate to see this country reduced once more to silly superstition.'

There was a flicker of anger on Bethesda's face, and Spleen smiled.

'If you think you can trick me into betraying my sisters, then you're a fool. I'll tell you nothing.'

'Of course you won't, but you'll tell Mr Gutterprod everything. He can be very persuasive. Your life, or death on the wheel. Is a mere friendship worth that?'

Spleen turned to leave. 'Do your worst, Mr Gutterprod,' he said. 'I shall be waiting in my office for your report. If she doesn't talk, then try to keep her alive. I don't wish to disappoint the crowds.' Spleen tapped the torturer once on the shoulder and swept out of the room, the mysterious sound of his feet following after.

Serrin placed the pen on his desk and looked kindly at his prisoner. This was the part he disliked, being Mr Nasty. He shrugged his shoulders as if to apologise for what was to come next, and then made a big show of struggling to open one of the drawers.

'It's nothing personal, you understand,' he said, withdrawing a large brass instrument and filling it carefully from a bottle marked

'Caustic – Only to be used when there's an 'R' in the month'.

'But someone has to do it, and why not me? Now, open your mouth wide, and say "arrgghh!"'

Tarantulus Spleen sat in his room, hidden in the shadows and staring at a silver hand mirror on the table.

'You think I'm vain, Mr Gutterprod. I can see it in your face.'

'No Sire, I think nothing of the sort – there's no shame in a man taking care of his appearance.'

'I assure you this mirror is quite useless. Here, you can see for yourself.'

Spleen leant forward into the light and slid the mirror across the polished surface of the table. Serrin protested.

'I was merely admiring the simplicity of its design, nothing more.'

'Pick it up Mr Gutterprod, it won't bite.'

Serrin's face turned from obsequious acceptance to surprise as he turned the mirror over in his hand.

'A sobering thought, is it not, Mr Gutterprod - to discover you don't exist.'

Serrin shivered and placed the mirror down quickly on the table. There'd been no reflection in the glass, nothing, just a black watery hole.

'There's no need for alarm. Your soul is quite safe. The mirror is a simple communication device, elegant as you say but unfortunately, silent.'

Spleen sat back in the shadows, and all Serrin could see of him were his fingers on the table and the rich embroidered surface of his robe. 'And what of your report?' Spleen asked. Serrin was dreading the question. He took out a few sheets of paper from his top pocket and glanced through them, using the time to gather his thoughts.

'For some strange reason,' he said after clearing his throat, 'you seem to be out-of-sorts with the Sisterhood, not popular at all. The prisoner was most adamant on the subject. It would appear they're planning a rebellion.' He paused and looked up from his notes, as though waiting for some dramatic gesture of surprise.

'You needn't look shocked, Mr Gutterprod. I would be insulted if the Sisterhood were acting any different. Please, continue - what of this Big Secret of theirs?'

Serrin eased the collar around his neck, feeling increasingly nervous about reading aloud from his notes. There were certain names the prisoner had called the sorcerer that he should have edited beforehand.

'The prisoner was less forthcoming about this. She needed more than the usual persuasion, sir. The words 'Mighty Mathog' and 'kicking your arse to kingdom come' were, if I recall, mentioned in the same sentence.'

Spleen laughed quietly to himself and tapped his gloved fingers together. 'We'd do well not to underestimate these women, if they count such a fabled beast as their friend.

'The great God Mathog indeed, will they ever learn.'

'There's more, Sire - some garbled reference to digging up worms, and a name – Hieronymus Beed. Utter dribble, a bait shop perhaps?'

The tapping fingers stopped.

'You have a short memory Mr Gutterprod, or else you're a fool. She means the prince.'

'Surely not, merely a coincidence, the boy's dead, you saw to it yourself…' Serrin stopped mid-sentence. It wasn't done to mention the murder of the royal family in the sorcerer's presence. He was innocent, and anyone suggesting otherwise had long since bounced off the cliffs for a snooze with the fishes.

'There's the faintest possibility the boy's still alive,' Spleen said, after an awkward silence. 'It would be unfortunate if the Sisterhood were hiding him. People have a fondness for the old family we shouldn't ignore.'

'News to me, Sire. You're nothing if not adored.'

'I'm feared, Mr Gutterprod, and rightly so. I'd have it no other way. This new development, though is cause for concern. 'Digging for worms,' did you say? There's much to think on here.'

'Is there?'

'You're a man of science, Mr Gutterprod. I suggest you use your imagination. I believe the prisoner was referring to the Great Wyrms of legend. It's hardly a difficult conclusion to make.'

'Then surely we've nothing to fear,' Serrin said, his professional pride hurt. 'Such creatures are a fanciful nonsense, a pretence of the old religion.'

The fingers started to tap on the table again.

'Yes, that may be, but Stench doesn't share your confidence.'

Serrin shrugged his shoulders. 'He's a simple creature…'

'But not so simple as to overlook the past. Tell me, Mr Gutterprod, as a man of science. How exactly do you think the Sisterhood escaped?'

'Magic, I suppose,'

'Ah, magic you say. A convenient answer, and one that would score well in an examination. But I think you overestimate the powers of these women. Even I can't fly to the stars.'

Spleen stood up from his chair and walked in front of the window, his large frame blocking out the light. 'What have you read of the ancient texts, Mr Gutterprod,' he asked staring out at the courtyard. 'Are they no longer taught in the Academy?'

'They're not popular, Sire, if that's what you mean.'

'A pity, you could learn much from these scripts. One, in particular, has proven invaluable to my research.' Spleen turned to face Serrin, his eyes glowing yellow through the holes in his mask. 'It was found in possession of a very foolish man, along with that mirror on the table.'

Serrin knew very well what foolish meant – resisting arrest at the hands of Stench's secret police.

'These communication devices are nothing more than tins tied together with invisible string, although I'm sure the Academy has a more convenient scientific explanation. No matter, their very existence points to one thing, holes in space.'

Serrin looked confused. He'd no idea what the sorcerer was talking about.

'And who made these holes, one may ask – although in your case I'm disappointed to see that you don't. The answer lies in the name - wyrmholes, Mr Gutterprod, wyrmholes. We pour scorn on the worship of Mathog, but there's truth in the old religion. Who are we to say that the Great Wyrms don't exist, that they never burrowed through space to leave tunnels in their wake?'

'But what has this to do with the Sisterhood?' Serrin asked. There was a lengthy silence before Spleen replied.

'I thought the conclusion obvious. They must know where these holes are, some of them at least. We stumbled across a few, courtesy of the unfortunate gentleman, but one of them is now shut – closed for ever, it seems.'

'How?'

'At last, a sensible question - by the same manner in which it was opened, I presume - by a Great Wyrm, and that makes the Sisterhood dangerous.'

'Why?'

'Because they can turn the worship of these creatures to their advantage. What better way of legitimising a rebellion than claiming it for a God.'

Spleen sat back in his chair and rubbed at a dry piece of skin under his mask. 'The old religion festers with these people, like an annoying itch. We live in a modern age. Sense and reason should suffice, not superstition. But it always comes down to this - one religion against another. If these women want their sordid little war, then we must oblige them, so long as it's not fought on our soil, eh Mr Gutterprod?'

Serrin nodded enthusiastically, his mind a blank.

'And if they raise one God, then it is only right and proper that I should destroy it with another. You've done well. Go back to your laboratory and prepare the woman for execution. I've no desire to deprive the old religion of a martyr.'

Spleen dismissed Serrin with a quick wave of his hand, and settled back to the safety of the shadows. So Stench's suspicions were correct. If the Sisterhood returned there'd be bloody rebellion, but that would never happen. He would make damned sure of that.

Spleen waited until the miserable Mr Gutterprod had bowed, fawned and scraped his way out of the office before bringing out a second mirror from under his robe, and laying it face up on the table. The surface of the glass shimmered as though it was a thin smear of oil.

'So,' said a voice, 'You have need of my help.'

Spleen pulled the mask from his head and ran his fingers through what was left of his hair. 'I think it's time we talked,' he said.

The four walls of the room seemed to twist out of shape as a figure stepped out of the ether, its hand outstretched in greeting. 'It will cost you dear, this agreement,' the figure said, and smiled with thin, pale lips as it gazed at the sorcerer.

Serrin closed the door quietly to his master's office. The meeting had gone well, far better than he had expected. He was still in one piece, a considerable achievement with the sorcerer's temper as changeable as the weather. That was the trouble with bad news, one had to learn to dress the words carefully. He allowed himself a brief chuckle of self-satisfaction then hurried back along the corridor to his laboratory. All he need do was sketch out the report, make sure the prisoner was looking her best for the morrow, and the rest of the morning would be his.

'Damn!' he cursed as he skidded to a halt. 'Some idiot's left a window open.'

A flock of angry seagulls blocked the way ahead, all snapping their beaks and making a mess on the polished floor. Serrin was not fond of birds, and from the way the creatures squinted at him with their yellow-rimmed eyes, it seemed the feeling was mutual. Serrin waved his arms and tried to shoo them away, and when this failed he peeled a candle from a window shelf and threw it at the nearest bird.

'Get out of it, you filthy creatures!' Serrin shouted. He may as well have scattered confetti for all the good it did. The birds turned to each other and began rattling their beaks, but this was no innocent conversation, no amusing ritual to keep a zoologist guessing. They were sharpening their beaks for an attack.

Serrin had hardly time to cover his eyes before the entire corridor turned white with flapping wings as the birds launched themselves at his head. He panicked, and pulling the collar of his coat above his ears, tripped and stumbled along the floor in his desperate attempts to shake them off. 'Can't you lend a hand?' he screamed as he made out the feet of a soldier standing outside the door to the laboratory. 'I'm being shredded to ribbons!' The guard stared straight ahead with his face set in an expression of mild indigestion, seemingly unconcerned. Serrin let out a squeal of anger. 'Oh, stand aside!' he snapped as he clawed at the handle, and the guard swung back with the door as it opened, the heels of his boots dragging on the parquet tiles.

Serrin pushed his way past and slammed the door shut, glad to be back in the safety of his laboratory, but the reason for the guard's peculiar behaviour was plain to see. The man had been speared to the woodwork from behind.

Serrin dropped on all fours and stifled a shriek of fear. Never brave at the best of times, he faced a terrifying quandary. On one side of the door blew a snowstorm of razor-sharp beaks, while on this side stalked a maniac who could pig-stick an oak door as though it was cardboard. And what if it was the prisoner? What if she'd managed to escape from her chains?

Serrin whimpered with indecision. Just my luck, he thought. She's definitely the sort who'd take things to heart. Another thought struck home too, more pressing than the first. His life wasn't worth a shellock if the prisoner was dead. It was worth even less if she was climbing down the drainpipe to escape. There was nothing for it, he would have to crawl round the corner and investigate.

Someone had set fire to the laboratory. A thick cloud of smoke was edging its way around the benches. Damn the morning and damn the day, it had been going far too well until now. Serrin felt his way between the furniture, and scuttled across to the nearest bench, hoping no one had heard. He looked over the top but could see nothing. He crept across to the opposite table but hit his head on a cupboard door. A large brass instrument rolled off the top before skewering itself deep in the torturer's buttock. Serrin fought back a cry of surprise, then looked over his shoulder at the big syringe sticking out from his trousers. At least it wasn't a spear, he thought and then felt his left leg go numb. 'Oh bugger!' he swore. 'Potion Number Five.'

A breeze of cool air struck him on the cheek, and through the thickening haze of smoke Serrin thought he could see the faint outline of an open window. He heaved himself forward and immediately knocked the side of another bench. He froze. There was the ominous sound of two more syringes rolling around above, and then one by one Serrin felt the inevitable stab of pain as the needles struck home. The grouping was perfect. Potion Number Seven, a little to the right of the bull's eye, caused a rush of toadstools to erupt along his spine. Potion Number Two, a little to the left of the outer ring, brought a feeling of sudden euphoria, and the need to confess all to anyone who would listen.

Serrin bit down on his tongue and slid as fast as he could towards the light, not caring what pieces of furniture he bumped into next. It was obvious the prisoner had escaped, two empty chains swung freely from the ceiling. He must raise

103

the alarm. Serrin pulled himself to his feet and with his left leg dragging behind him, staggered the last few steps towards the open window. 'Guards!' he shouted at the top of his voice, 'look to the walls!' Across the courtyard, he could see a tall figure, all covered in rags, stride purposely forward with the unmistakeable outline of Bethesda Chubb draped across its shoulders.

'Guards!' was what he had intended to say. What came out of his mouth was entirely different. As Serrin pointed to the figure escaping over the battlements, the guards in the courtyard looked up at the torturer, hardly believing their ears. Potion Number 2 had kicked in, and the helpless Serrin Gutterprod was paralysed with honesty, kissing goodbye to his pension and any chance of surviving the week by shouting to the heavens what he thought of his Master, those effeminate robes, the rats, and where exactly the sorcerer could stick his job.

Chapter Six

It was the curse of the academic, to be an authority on trivia yet a stranger to common sense, and Professor Arbutus Broadbent was no exception. He could wax lyrical for hours about a small patch of lichen on a gravel path, but tell him to step aside and let the wedding party pass, and he would look at you dumbfounded. It was the same with physics. 'Fascinating isn't it,' he stuttered, his teeth chattering in the cold, 'to be so near the sun and yet f-f-frozen to the core. Not what one would expect at all. And to think I was under the misapprehension that clouds were p-p-puffs of steam. I shall write a pamphlet on this very subject when I return.'

Arabella couldn't think why, the professor's observations seemed singularly unsurprising but then she was a witch and used to flying. She declined to state the obvious, not from any sense of politeness, but from a heartfelt certainty that if she tried to open her mouth her lips would tear apart. That was the trouble with travelling at speed on the back of a wyrm. She felt a breath of warm air condense on the back of her neck as the professor thought of another interesting observation.

'And no birds, Miss Pike. Have you noticed that?'

Of course, there were no birds, thought Arabella. Only a fool would be flying high above the clouds on a morning like this, and curse Her Majesty for insisting they did. She heard the sound of linen-backed paper flap and crackle as Professor Broadbent decided foolishly to unfold the map and see where they were. 'Man overboard!' she shouted at Her Majesty.

'Not again?'' sighed the wyrm, and dived down after the unfortunate professor for the fourth time.

You could have heard a barometer drop in the dining hall of Grubdale Towers as the hungry boys watched their headmaster raise a fork to his mouth. There had been a third case of food poisoning in the school, and this time it was poor Mr Gammon's chair that stood empty. It was too much for the cook. She stormed out of the kitchen and stood in the centre of the hall as the boys toyed with their food, her face flushed with anger and her hands holding a large frying pan as though facing a serve at tennis. It was a question of professional pride. 'If people smuggle food into school then they get what they deserve,' she protested at the top of her voice. 'Now eat up, every one of you! There's nothing wrong with my cooking, and heaven help the next person that turns green!'

It was not perhaps the best of menus with which to make a principled stand. The pale orange mush was obviously boiled swede, but the lumps of meat in the stew were a taxonomic mystery. It was the end of the month, and anything that scuttled about on four legs could be called a calorie when the cupboards were bare. The cook was adamant, confidence was to be restored. She stared angrily at the headmaster, and from the way she was swinging the frying pan, was in no mood to accept excuses.

'Now then boys,' Mr Withers said. 'You heard Cook — there's nothing to be frightened from a little bit of gristle. Continue with your meal.' But despite his brave words, Mr Withers was making heavy work of backing them up with any action. Three cases of food poisoning in less than a month were enough to hang Mrs Beaton. He raised the fork a second time and tried to convince his lips to open, but it was futile. His tongue was stuck securely to the roof of his mouth, and not even a chocolate éclair would have induced him to dribble.

'Here, pass it over then if you're not hungry,' Rowena Carp, said leaning rudely across the table and helping herself to the headmaster's plate. 'I'm famished.' She'd been cleaning her ears with the corner of her handkerchief and had missed all the commotion.

'It looks delicious as usual, Cook. Well done,' Rowena said, spooning Mr Wither's portion on top of her own, and tucking the handkerchief under her chin like a bib. 'Well, here goes, eye's down for a full house,' and oblivious to all the faces staring at her from about the room, Rowena attacked her meal with gusto, stopping only occasionally to suck air in through her pursed lips as if to emphasise how deliciously scrumptious it all was. With a sigh of relief the boys followed suit, their hunger getting the better of them, but caution still reigned supreme at the staff table, and to Rowena's surprise, plate after plate was emptied into hers. 'Come now, Mr Doggerel, you'll be getting me fat,' she teased, but on seeing him waver, Rowena grabbed his meal and continued to eat.

'A monument to digestion you are, Miss Carp,' whispered the headmaster, 'and a timely one at that. What do you say Dr Brent?' The new music teacher was saying nothing. Private Oldfield was looking on in horror as the enemy shovelled forkful after forkful of slops down her face.

'Why don't you give Miss Carp your plate, Hildegard dear,' whispered Rufus Doggerel, tapping Private Oldfield gently on the hand. 'Trust me, you'll feel better for it afterwards.' He looked around to make sure the headmaster wasn't listening. 'I find I work better on an empty stomach where the Cook's concerned,' he continued, 'particularly at the end of the month.'

Private Oldfield squirmed under the padding of his disguise and lifted the English teacher's hand from his own. 'Good idea,' he mouthed, pushing his plate towards Miss Carp as though it was a bomb waiting to explode. Rowena belched and winked at him, an unfortunate habit that brought forth terrible memories of his tussle in the broom cupboard back at the Alpine Palace. Could it be the damned woman recognised him under the wig and wintergreen? No, it was impossible. Mr Doggerel was playing footsie under the table and leering at him in such a suggestive manner a quick slap was in order.

The cook seeing the boys tuck into their evening meal, had retreated in satisfaction to the kitchen, her pride restored. Mr Withers made the best use of this opportunity to retire to his office. There was the question of yet another vacancy to be filled, and like before the agency was most efficient and disturbingly quick in offering a replacement. It was as though they'd known about the unfortunate poisonings before they'd even happened. But that would be ridiculous.

Mr Withers sat down at his desk and unwrapped a delicious ham and egg pie from his secret drawer before looking over the latest curriculum vitae that had arrived by afternoon post. It concerned a certain Herr Bombast who, on paper at least, seemed just the sort of athletic young man the school needed. He lost little time in writing to the agency and employing the gentleman on the spot, beggars after all could not be choosers, and a bit of Teutonic discipline could do no harm, particularly with Bede. The mysterious boy had been acting strange recently, parading himself around the school as though he was royalty.

It wasn't just Bede's behaviour that had changed since Rowena had joined the staff, Squint too was acting peculiar. He was having feelings, awkward feelings - the sort of feelings that cold showers are supposed to stop, yet a quick rub with the soap and flannel seem to encourage. To put it politely, as Rufus Doggerel was trying to explain to Rowena that evening in the staffroom, he was like a 'bull in a knocking shop.'

'May I speak plainly, Miss Carp, as a friend and fellow teacher?'

'Please do,' answered Rowena, blissfully unaware of the sudden change in conversation, and dipping a ginger biscuit in her cup of rum tea. She made room for him on the battered sofa. Mr Doggerel squeezed in next to her and spoke quietly out of the side of his mouth.

'There's a whiff of tomcat about the boy's dormitory that's becoming difficult to ignore,' he said.

Rowena popped the sodden biscuit in her mouth and sucked each of her fingers in turn. 'And what has that to do with me?' she asked with a hint of annoyance in her voice. 'I'm not the school cleaner. My contract states quite clearly I am here to teach.'

'I meant nothing of the kind, dear Rowena, and heaven help me if I did. What I'm trying to say, in the most delicate way possible, is that we must tread carefully where one of our boys is concerned. We seem to have a new rooster in the chicken coop.'

'Oh I shouldn't worry about that,' Rowena said after some moments thought. 'Mr Withers explained everything to me when I first arrived. He approves of the older boys having pets.'

'Does he, by Jove!' exclaimed Mr Doggerel grasping the wrong end of the stick altogether. 'That way leads to ruin!'

Rowena bristled with contempt. 'I see nothing wrong in adopting one of nature's creatures as a companion. Dear Demetrios here has been a great comfort to me over the years.'

It was obvious to Mr Doggerel that delicate metaphors were wasted on the lady. He decided to be blunt. 'We seem to be talking at cross purposes,' he said. 'I'm trying to warn you about Squint, so let us not be coy. It's my considered opinion the lad has taken to adolescence like a duck to water.'

'Meaning?'

'Oh come now, Miss Carp. You're a teacher of science, and I'm a man of the world. Do we need to spell it out? The boy's an absolute sewer. Of course usually it wouldn't be a problem. A few withering verses from the Old Testament, or a two-mile swim in the freezing waters of the canal would suffice but in his case…'

'I think I get the picture,' interrupted Rowena, looking frantically around the room to see if anyone was listening.

'The trouble is Miss Carp, now we have female members of staff the situation's changed. Given the appearance of that trout Dr Brent, I rather feel it's you who should be on the lookout.'

'But he's only a boy.'

'He's eighteen if a day.'

'What? Then he shouldn't be at school!"

'I agree with you wholeheartedly, but what can we do? Mr Withers insists the boy's a slow developer. Not a conclusion I share. His writing makes the walls of the gentleman's washrooms at Piccadilly read like poetry. You see my concern?'

Rowena admitted she could. Squint's behaviour in class had changed from merry disobedience to such a disturbing infatuation that leaning over the boy's shoulder to check his spelling was like playing Russian roulette with a dictionary. 'But what should I do?' she asked.

'Lock your bedroom door for one thing. The sooner we get this boy out of school and into a job with The Firm the better. In the meantime there are certain powders I believe that may come in useful.'

'Well, there is one herb…'

Rowena took Mr Doggerel's advice to heart. She had locked the bedroom door before getting into bed, leant the back of the chair under the handle, and instead of slipping into her thick cotton nightdress had put on so many layers of clothing that her wardrobe was almost empty. 'From tonight Demetrios you can sleep on my bed,' she said slipping down between the sheets and pulling them tight underneath her chin. 'Let nothing past the counterpane, especially in pyjamas. Now be a good sport and blow out the candle.'

Demetrios did as he was told and jumped on board, making the most of his new sleeping arrangements by shuffling around in a circle until he was comfortable. But Rowena was far from settled. Her stomach was fighting a rearguard action with the boiled swede. She was too hot with her clothes on, then too cold with the sheets flung back, but above all she was nervous of the noises coming from outside her door. Common sense would have told her they were the scratching of mice, or else the creaking of floorboards as they shrunk with the cold, but common sense was nowhere that night. In its place was the image of a passion-crazed Squint straining at the hinges with a crowbar. She placed a pillow over her head and trusted her safety to the jaws of Demetrios.

Rowena woke a few hours later to the sound of her loyal guardian chasing rabbits in his sleep and the rattle of a door handle in the background. There was no mistaking the noise this time. Someone was trying to get into her room. She flung herself out of bed and kicking the chair aside, stood with all her weight against the door. 'Who is it?' she hissed. 'Damn it Squint, is that you?'

There was no reply from the other side, but Rowena was convinced she could hear heavy breathing. She crouched down to look through the keyhole as the handle gave another shake.

'I can tell it's you, Squint. Now go back to bed before you get into serious trouble.'

Someone laughed. It was the last straw. Rowena jumped quickly to her feet and took out her key. 'There are more things in heaven and earth,' she preached as she unlocked the door and flung it aside, 'than are dreamt of in your underpants...'

'How quaint, Shakespeare and at this hour of the morning.'

Rowena found herself staring open-mouthed at the figure of Dr Hildegard Brent.

'I thought I'd wake you up with a nice cup of tea, seeing as you've missed breakfast. The headmaster was getting worried, what with the recent tummy-troubles. May I come in?'

Before Rowena had time to answer, Private Oldfield made a great show of squeezing past and placing a mug of hot tea on the bedside table, but not before sneaking the key from out of the door and into his pocket. 'No biscuits I'm afraid,' he said, sitting down on a chair by the window and remembering to keep his legs together, 'but then we ladies must look after our figures.'

Rowena frowned, thinking this a barbed comment. She was still dressed in multi-layers of clothing and spilling out between the buttons.

'I'm glad I've caught you on your own, Miss Carp. I've been looking forward to a cosy chat, just us girls together.' Private Oldfield winced from embarrassment. He still hadn't mastered the part and was beginning to sound like a frustrated wallflower the night before a dance.

'It was kind of you to bring me a cup of tea,' Rowena said, 'but as you can tell, I'm late for class. Perhaps we could talk some other time?'

Private Oldfield was more than relieved, he was in the room for one reason only, and the sooner the task was finished, the better. 'I'm sorry,' he said. 'I should have realised. What must you think of me?' He rose to leave then pretended to pick something off the floor. 'You've dropped your door key. I'd look after it if I were you.' He placed it into Rowena's hand and hurried off down the stairs, making sure that the square of soft clay in which he had made the impression was tucked safely away in his pocket.

'Oh, there you are Miss Carp,' spluttered an agitated Mr Gartside clutching the latest addition to the school silver to his chest as he waited outside the classroom. 'I tried to keep the boys amused, but I'm afraid they're a little restless.' Mr Gartside was the oldest member of the teaching staff and hated excitement of any sort. From the look of his pale, sweaty face as he waited for Rowena to take over, he'd had more than

113

what was good for him that morning. 'It doesn't do to leave them alone for too long,' he said making a show of looking at his watch. 'It doesn't do at all.' The poor man had just taken the class for 'Evaluation' and had made the terrible mistake of short-changing the boys over a Georgian teapot. The door to the classroom shook on its hinges as something large hit the woodwork. Mr Gartside jumped with fear. 'Too much treacle in their porridge,' he said as he shuffled away in his carpet slippers. 'I've warned Cook about this thing before. It's not my fault.'

Rowena took five deep breaths, rolled up her sleeves and swung the door open with a mighty slam. She'd slept poorly, had missed breakfast and was in no mood to take prisoners. 'What is this noise?' she shouted as she marched into the room. 'Sit down at your desks at once!' The class was in an uproar over the sudden downturn in the price of silver. 'I said be quiet!' she roared, not that it had any effect. The boys were fighting with each other over who said yes to Gartside's derisory offer. Pursglove, it seemed, had advised caution throughout, although no one could remember him saying a word. Mellor, on the other hand, resented being called a 'thick biscuit' and denied offering out his hand and saying 'Spit on it, it's a deal.' As far as Mellor was concerned it was Spiggot who'd sealed the contract. The boy was a sugar addict desperate for his weekly allowance. Rowena tried to stop two of the boys from smashing chairs over each other's heads, but even a well-aimed kick failed to bring them to order. Something flew past her ear. Instinctively she reached out her hand and grabbed the object before it hit the floor - it was Mildew.

The expression on Rowena's face spoke of boilers bulging outwards and arrows pointing to the red. 'Who threw this

114

boy?' she shouted, holding up the poor embarrassed Mildew by his greasy shirt collar. 'I demand to be told. I will not have this sort of behaviour in my classroom!' None of the boys had the sense to answer. It was the last straw. There was an almighty BANG as though a bomb had been thrown into the room, and in an instant the floor cleared as the class scampered under their desks for cover. Rowena blew the smoke away from the tip of her forefinger and held Mildew as far away from her as possible. The poor boy was petrified and had started to drip childishly on the floor. She looked down at the scared white faces peeking out from under the desks and smiled. 'I want you to sit down at your desks, not under them,' she said in a calm, matter-of-fact voice.

'But that noise Miss, what was it?'

'Noise, Pursglove? I heard nothing but shouting. Now get up all of you. I've no intention of taking this lesson sitting crossed-legged on the floor.'

Rowena let go of Mildew's collar and ushered him into a seat. 'Come on, I haven't all day,' she said. 'Honestly, I don't know what's gotten into you. You're as excitable as a piglet in a field of sausages. From now on I want complete silence when I enter the room. It's what we call 'manners'.'

There was a nervous shuffling of the chairs as the class resumed their seats. It was perhaps best under the circumstances to concede defeat. The door to the classroom opened, and a worried Private Oldfield looked in. 'Is everything all right?' he asked, out of breath from dashing down the corridor.

'Everything is fine, Dr Brent. Why do you ask?'

Private Oldfield looked around the room and readjusted the grey wig on his head. 'There was a bang?'

115

'Was there? I can't say I noticed. Did any of you boys hear anything?'

The expression on Rowena's face, as she asked the question, ensured the correct response. There was a collective shaking of heads, with one notable exception.

'She's got a gun,' said Bede before being hit on the head by Squint from behind.

Rowena was horrified. 'Don't talk such rubbish, Bede. That imagination of yours will get you into trouble. Ignore the boy, Dr Brent. He's trying to be funny. No doubt you heard Cook dropping pans in the kitchen. It's not been a good month for her, all things considered.'

Private Oldfield was unconvinced and studied Bede's face closely. He'd definitely heard a gun of some sort being fired.

'Please Dr Brent, if you don't mind. I'm trying to take class. After all, you don't see me barging in on one of your lessons unannounced.'

Private Oldfield retreated from the door and closed it quietly behind him, knowing full well that he'd been stone-walled by that horrid woman. Here was another mystery to solve. Miss Carp was teaching the boys to use firearms.

'Bede, I'm very disappointed with you,' Rowena said after Dr Brent had left the room. 'Are you trying to get me into trouble?'

'Yeah, hairy arse,' Squint said, adding to the debate. 'What do you think you're playing at? Do you want the coppers poking their noses around? You know what The Firm would make of that.'

The boys looked knowingly at each other at the mention of The Firm, and some even ran fingers across their throats in a suggestive manner. Bede remained silent.

'I shouldn't worry about Bede, Miss,' Squint said. 'He's off his head, thinks he's too good for the likes of us. Go on you little runt, tell Miss Carp how you're a prince.'

'But I am!' shouted Bede, slamming his fist down on the top of his desk, and the rest of the class laughed and jeered at the miserable boy.

Private Oldfield was no locksmith, but there were certain lessons he'd picked up over the course of the afternoon. Molten lead, for instance, when poured into a damp clay mould tends to spit like a cornered tomcat, burn holes through the thickest of surgical stockings, and when cool is surprisingly hot to touch. It is also useless for making keys, being about as rigid as a boiled baby carrot. A metal file, on the other hand, was just the ticket. All one needed was a suitable blank, three hours of endless rubbing and a bowl of warm water to bathe the swollen wrist in - optional activities if after sneaking up to the room in question the door opens of its own accord. A lesser man would have cried. Private Oldfield swore and rolled a stale pork pie along the floor, just in case anything pink and rabid was hiding under the bed.

'Miss Carp, are you in?' he asked as a final precaution, and hearing no reply entered Rowena's room. He checked the small cupboard first, rattling open the drawer and emptying its contents on the bed, but could find only empty sweet wrappers and a small bundle of toothpicks. He scooped them back in the drawer and looked for somewhere else to search. The suitcase by the chair revealed nothing of interest except a racy novel and a picture of a Scottish Highlander with his kilt blowing in the breeze. A romantic memento no doubt given the pathetic message scrawled at the bottom…

To ma wee timorous beastie
Angus McRavish
XXXX

...but hardly incriminating. The wardrobe was next; a mysterious cave of femininity with pockets galore to rummage through. Perhaps a shoulder holster and a supply of bullets? But no, only more sweets and toffee. Really, thought Private Oldfield, the woman must have teeth of iron, which she did, her spare upper set cutting deep into Private Oldfield's fingers as he delved inside a large flannel dressing gown. He let out a brief cry of pain before shoving his fingers in his mouth and looking for something suitable to bandage his wound. This will have to do, he thought as he wrapped a voluminous silk garment around his hand, and got down on all fours to wipe away the drops of blood. Can't have the woman thinking she's been burgled. He remembered the porkpie. Better pick that up too, he thought, before noticing a great bite taken out of its crust.

It was as though the cold wooden floor had become a trampoline. Private Oldfield performed the perfect back somersault and landed on the bed. That damned woman's dog was somewhere in the room.

To say that Jellicoes eat anything is an understatement, and Demetrios was no exception. His diet had been one endless trail of extinction throughout the forests of Tweeb, but one bite of a four-week-old meat pie had been enough. Demetrios spat the offending mould and gristle from his mouth and crawled out from under the wardrobe. Someone was trying to poison him.

Private Oldfield panicked. 'Nice dog,' he whispered, pressing his back up against the wall in an attempt to shrink away from the beast. 'Who's a good dog then?'

Not Demetrios obviously, for the Jellico turned an unnerving shade of purple and started to creep around the bed like a tiger in the long grass intent on pudding.

'Sit, stay…no, get off the sheets!' pleaded Private Oldfield. He took one look at Demetrios' curled lip, cursed his stupidity then rolled quickly off the bed as the pink 'poodle' pounced. It was a timely escape. He sat horrified on the floor as Demetrios reduced the pillow to a cloud of feathers. But something had caught his attention. Demetrios' front feet were standing on a brown envelope that looked suspiciously important. Gathering all the courage he could muster, Private Oldfield reached out and snatched the envelope causing Demetrios to flip sideways and land on his back. It was like a scene from a slapstick comedy where the waiter whisks away the tablecloth and leaves the crockery intact, except in this case the Sunday china was a slavering beast making a frightening impression of an upturned turtle. Private Oldfield gathered his skirt between his legs and made a run for the stairs, slamming and locking the door shut behind him. This mission was becoming decidedly dangerous, he thought, and out of sheer spite mewed like a cat. It was a defiant but foolish thing to do, and Private Oldfield regretted his mistake as with a crash, Demetrios flung himself at the flimsy panelling and tried to scratch his way through. Private Oldfield took his cue to hurry down the stairs and move his bed in front of the door, but the risk had been worth taking. Captain Dashing would be pleased. He had snatched from the feet of the enemy a most useful piece of information, a photograph of the flying machine, or as the vicar thought, a dragon.

There had been an unfortunate misunderstanding at the top of the North tower. Demetrios had taken a bite out of Rowena's leg, and Rowena had kicked Demetrios over the wardrobe, all because the woman had stumbled into the room unannounced. The two of them sat at opposite ends of the bed and sulked. Rowena was feeling particularly sorry for herself. Bede was a worry, Squint a liability and she had made the mistake of relying on crude magic to keep her class in order. The last thing Rowena wanted was an argument. 'I don't know what you're so aggrieved about,' she moaned, rubbing her ankle and checking for puncture wounds. 'It was a hurtful thing to do, attacking me like that as though I was a common criminal.'

Demetrios snorted with anger and looked the other way.

'I'm sorry if I left you on your own, but that's no excuse for this kind of behaviour. You're getting nasty and spiteful in your old age. I should have got you seen to earlier.'

Demetrios raised his eyes in contempt. Not that old chestnut again.

'Spare the scissors and spoil the furniture, that's what I say.'

'Yeah, yeah, yeah…' thought Demetrios.

Rowena stepped out of her dress and walked to the wardrobe.

'And if you think I'm letting you sleep on the bed after this little performance then you're mistaken,' she moaned. 'You should count yourself lucky you're not spending the night outside in the cold. See how generous I am.' Her voice became muffled as she searched amongst the clothes for her nightdress. Demetrios yawned and walked to the other end of the bed, then from sheer bloody-mindedness lay down and made himself comfortable.

'Very funny, I don't think!' Rowena said as she pulled the thick cotton nightdress over her head. 'I'll give you until a count of three to get down from there.' She leant back inside the wardrobe for her dressing gown. 'One…'

Demetrios put his tongue out behind her back.

'Two…'

Demetrios' resolve began to waiver. There was a pair of slippers in the wardrobe, and his backside ached as it was.

'Three! Oh, Demetrios, how could you, you've been rummaging through my pockets for sweets!'

Demetrios' expression was the nearest thing to 'duh!' as he could manage.

'As though I don't feed you enough. And what else have you been up to?' Rowena complained as she searched for further evidence of misdemeanours in her wardrobe. 'Have you gone through my drawers as well?' This last comment was meant to be sarcastic but was nearer to the truth than she imagined. 'Wait a minute, something's missing here. Where are my best silken bloomers?' Rowena slammed the door shut in disgust and looked accusingly at her companion. 'If I find you've ripped them to shreds along with my pillow,' she said wagging her finger. 'Then I'll tan the…' She stopped mid-sentence. There were certain inconsistencies in her reasoning. Take mathematics, for instance, if x = one pink Jellico barely two feet tall and y = a wardrobe handle 5 feet from the floor, then $x + y$ could mean only one thing - some filthy pervert had run off with her winter bloomers. 'Oh Demetrios!' she cried realising her mistake. 'We've been burgled, and I bet I know the culprit, that damned sewer of a lad, Squint!'

Downstairs on the third floor Private Oldfield had a restless sleep. It was as though the person in the room above was rearranging the furniture and stacking it against the door.

Chapter Seven

At a mud-splattered crossroads somewhere across the Welsh border, a question of geography was being discussed.

'No Miss Pike, I am not trying to be facetious,' Professor Broadbent said. 'I'm sure your pronunciation is perfect, but if you wouldn't mind repeating the name again. I can't seem to find it on the map.'

Arabella shook the ice crystals from her hair and cast a knowing look at Her Majesty. The professor's near-death experience had done little to clear his mind. She shone the torch at the sign post and tried to make sense of the faded letters. That was the trouble with the Welsh language, too many consonants and not enough vowels. She took a deep breath and attempted to read out what must have taken a sign writer half a day to paint.

'A fascinating people, the Welsh,' the professor said after waiting for Arabella to pick her dentures up from the ground. 'One would have thought from all those letters, that we stand before a citadel, not some tiny village. Why, it hardly warrants a mention on the map. Try reading out the other name, it looks shorter.'

Arabella tried her best.

'Excellent Miss Pike,' the professor said after wiping the syllables from his face. 'It's as I thought, we're lost. Here, see for yourself. We've landed in a veritable desert. It's as though the Ordinance Survey took one look at this place and called it a day.'

Arabella looked over the professor's shoulder and flicked an icicle off his ear to see the map more clearly. 'What about that clump of trees in the left-hand corner?' she asked prodding the paper with her finger. 'Didn't we fly over a forest? Surely that must have a name?'

Professor Broadbent screwed up his face and peered at the map through watery eyes. 'Canada,' he mumbled after some consideration. Arabella's patience was as thin as the cold night air.

'Canada, you say? Well, dare I suggest it's your map at fault and not my pronunciation? The scale's all wrong. You'd be hard pressed to find your way to London with that, let alone 'Cloggy-noggy what-ever-you-call-it.'

'Yes, well I admit you have a point, but you could've been a teeny bit more tactful. What do you suggest? Asking someone for directions?'

'At this time of night with a giant wyrm poking her nose through someone's curtains? I hardly think that wise. No Professor, I suggest we re-trace our steps and follow the night-train to Holyhead.'

'And what then may I ask?'

'I thought that would be obvious,' Arabella said climbing back onto the wyrm's neck. 'We turn left at the sound of a chapel choir and fly straight on till we bump into Snowdon!'

124

Captain Hilary Dashing was finding it difficult to hide his excitement. There was a smile on his face and a skip in his step as he walked up and down the linoleum. Behind two polished doors that led off from the corridor, important men in smart tailored suits were spilling coffee and choking on cigars as they read each page of his report. It had come as no surprise, the telegram demanding his immediate presence in London. As soon as he'd handed the report to the motorcycle courier, slapping the rear mudguard as though it was a horse, he knew the cogs of some unstoppable machine had been set in action. He'd gone over the head of his superior and addressed the package to the Prime Minister.

'Would you like a cup of tea?' asked one of those nameless civil servants who haunt the corridors of power, hurrying from one office to another carrying files and boxes or else waving pieces of paper in the air as if to dry the ink. Captain Dashing took his ear away from the door and shook his head.

'No, thank you. I'll wait here if you don't mind. I'm sure they'll be finished soon.'

'And you are?' the civil servant asked, remembering something about security procedures.

'Captain Hilary Dashing.'

The civil servant looked impressed and fluttered his hand in front of his face. 'Not the Captain Dashing?' he said as he walked away. The heroic soldier straightened the buttons on his jacket and checked the sit of his peaked cap, not understanding what the civil servant meant, but feeling suitably proud. The poor captain, his surname was infamous at the war office. A careless answer to the calculated question - 'Isn't that man over there Dashing?' – had spelt the end of many a security risk in the secret service. It was less obvious than having to ask awkward questions, or getting the doorman to blow kisses at a new recruit.

The captain took out his pocket watch and checked the time, cursing his impatience. He'd been kept waiting in the corridor for nearly an hour. Perhaps it was a good sign. His last meeting had lasted only minutes, about as long it took for his first report to slide off the table and into the bin, a reflection of its flimsy content. His new report included so much meat and detail that even the greediest of minds would be happy. He smiled to himself as he placed the watch back in his jacket. What a fortuitous week it had been, and he owed it all to a drunken vicar and a photograph smuggled to him through a privet bush in the grounds of Grubdale Towers. His report concerned the strange disappearance of the double agent Frauline Charlie and the simultaneous arrival of those women in tweed at the Alpine Palace. It hardly took a genius to realise the connection. For the facts of the case were these – the women were obviously German. The captain was a fan of Wagner and could spot a Brunhilda from a Nelly Dean even with his opera glasses steamed up. The women had known the correct response to Private Oldfield's coded greeting, and they had tried to assassinate the poor fellow in a broom cupboard. There could be only one conclusion. Frauline Charlie had discovered something of such terrible importance that she had been bumped off, and the captain had a good idea of what that something was – a planned uprising, revolution! Scattered throughout his beloved country were cells of these formidable women stirring up trouble between the suffragettes and the police, and according to Private Oldfield, arming impressionable teenagers with guns.

The captain had to admit there were certain parts of his report difficult to swallow. But the camera never lies, as the vicar had once said, giving two girls in his congregation an excellent idea and newspapers around the world the first pictures of a goblin on a toadstool and some fairies frolicking in a wood. The photographs in the report suggested a campaign of terror, a cabal of women preying on the superstitious minds of innocent country folk by appearing as witches. Just like the Germans to try and frighten people with their Brothers Grimm, he thought and gave the side of his cavalry boot a swipe with his cane. He struck it a second and third time, trying to block out the memory of a particularly horrifying fairy tale his mother used to read to him at night. But the situation in Derbyshire was more terrible than anything a child could imagine. Here witches were tangibly real and armed to the teeth with shotguns and high explosive. Take the village of Sodden already under their spell, its inhabitants little more than zombies walking the streets as though nothing had happened. At least the captain had the sense to visit the place and photograph the ruined street with the church split down the middle and liable to collapse at any minute. And he was no fool. He had left the best of the photographs to last, a picture of a terrifying German flying machine called der Wurm.

The doors to the conference room swung open, and a gentleman in a dark grey suit appeared at the captain's side. 'If you would be so kind as to come in,' he said. 'The Prime Minister is ready to see you.'

The captain recovered from the shock of being tapped rudely on the shoulder, puffed out his chest as if to show off his medals and pushed past. 'Well?' he asked excitedly after sitting down at a large mahogany table and sizing up the situation with one look. 'Am I mad, or is the country in trouble?'

'Both,' said the Prime Minister after a moment of considered silence, 'but primarily, I think the latter.

'To be brief Captain Dashing,' he continued, 'there are certain aspects of your report I find disturbing. If what you've written is true, then German technology has advanced far beyond our own capabilities, if not the limits of science. Giant airships we accept but when someone talks of flying witches and fire-breathing dragons we must sit up and take notice.'

The captain fidgeted in his seat, unsure if he was being made fun of, or not. 'All I can tell you Prime Minister is what I saw with my own eyes.'

'Harrumph!' snorted one of the grey-suited gentlemen seated at the table and trying not to laugh. The Prime Minister smiled and patted him on the sleeve. 'Please let the Captain continue, Charles. We are not all gifted with your sense of clarity. I for one am keeping an open mind.' He tapped the photograph of the great wyrm with his finger. 'You say you saw this creature land on Grimspittle moor?' he asked.

'Yes, Prime Minister.'

'And that it attacked you and Private Oldfield without provocation?'

'Without provocation and with deadly intent, just as I have written.'

'Quite, I am merely trying to establish the facts. There is one point that puzzles me, though. This photograph of the dragon, our only piece of evidence; it appears somewhat familiar.'

'It does?' exclaimed Captain Dashing. 'You mean to say you've seen such machines before?' There was an embarrassed silence as knowing glances were exchanged around the table.

'Not exactly, but something quite like it. I too have a photograph.' The Prime Minister reached inside his jacket pocket and flung a piece of card across the table.

'But this is incredible!' Captain Dashing said, turning the card over and gasping with astonishment. 'Another contraption! The person who took this photograph deserves a medal. Why, it's a wonder he wasn't crushed to death.'

Not everyone in the room was of the same opinion. The captain raised his head to see two or more gentlemen trying not to giggle. 'Wait a minute,' he said. 'I know what's going on. This is one of our own, isn't it? Hah! I knew we were as good as the Germans.'

There was no pretence of hiding the laughter anymore; the room was in an uproar.

'What did I say that was so funny?' the captain asked, upset at this reaction.

The Prime Minister raised his hand and called the meeting to order. 'Don't you see? This photograph is a postcard. It's of a statue in Regents Park - a concrete dinosaur. How do I know your photograph isn't the same, some holiday souvenir?'

'No,' Captain Dashing said, raising himself up from the chair. 'I don't agree. What I saw on Grimspittle moor was no statue!'

'And neither was it a dragon, come on man, be reasonable.'

'But I never said it was. That's my whole point. What landed on the moor could only have been a flying machine, and if it wasn't our own, then I think we should be worried.'

The Prime Minister stared at the captain for a very long time. 'And that's why we've called you here today,' he said in a slow matter-of-fact voice. 'Only a comedian or a very honest man could have written this report. Please have the courtesy to resume your seat.' He nodded towards a gentleman seated at his left, one who had been conspicuous in not laughing. The man got up from the chair and pulled down a chart on the opposite wall. On it was painted a large black silhouette.

'This is Mr Jennings, Captain Dashing; a very clever man here at the Ministry. You should listen to what he has to say. You may be pleasantly surprised.'

Mr Jennings tapped the chart with his finger. 'Look closely at the picture and tell me the first thoughts that come to mind,' he said.

'So that's it, you do think I'm mad!'

'Do as Mr Jennings says Captain,' urged the Prime Minister.

Captain Dashing scratched his head. He'd been tested like this before. At least this time the ink blot looked nothing like his mother in a grass skirt pulling turnips from a field. He screwed up his face and stared at the picture through half-closed eyes. 'A black crow?' he suggested.

Mr Jennings smiled. 'Interesting,' he said. 'I would have described it as an eagle.'

Damn, thought the captain, here we go again. He decided to brave it out. 'I don't understand,' he said.

'The picture on the chart is a silhouette of the latest German flying machine. It is called a Taube, which is German for dove, a sweet name for something so deadly. We think it's this you saw on Grimspittle moor.'

The captain sighed with relief. He was believed at last. 'I suppose it could look like a dragon, but it would depend on its size and colour.'

The Prime Minister nodded towards Mr Jennings. 'The statistics please,' he asked. Mr Jennings cleared his throat and proceeded to point out various details.

'It is our belief that the Taube represents a significant improvement in aircraft design. Note its sleek appearance as seen from the ground, the large sweeping wings, and the tail fins for instance. Recent intelligence indicates it to be a two-seater monoplane, far larger than anything we have in development. It's quite possible the plane can fly for considerable distances without refuelling, and at some speed. We've been outclassed gentlemen. Our own designs are nothing compared to this.'

The captain looked pleased with himself. 'But can it breathe fire?' he asked.

'That would be most unwise Captain, considering the plane's construction. But you have a point. We should not discount the possibility of some form of explosive weaponry. We know of at least one occasion where such ordinance was used.'

Everyone in the room looked shocked. 'You mean to say that someone can drop grenades from these machines?' asked one of the grey-suited gentlemen.

'It was tried with some success in Mexico, I believe. But not with a plane of this size.'

'The swines!' interrupted the captain. 'And there I was blaming it on Pluggham and Splatter!'

The Prime Minister looked confused.

'I think the Captain is referring to the explosion on Grimspittle moor,' Mr Jennings said. 'It was most probably a bomb.'

'Heavens, then none of our cities are safe!'

'Unfortunately Prime Minister, that's my conclusion too. Germany has airships capable of delivering the same, but a fast, sleek bomber is something new, something terrible. It represents a significant threat.'

'Especially if the damn thing's on British soil. What is Germany up to?'

131

Mr Jennings shrugged his shoulders. 'That is for anyone to decide, but you see gentlemen, we shouldn't laugh at the Captain. He has made a terrible discovery. The presence of German warplanes over British soil is of major concern.'

'But what of these 'flying' women?' the Prime Minister insisted. 'How do you boffins account for those? Are they machines too?'

'Ah yes, the infamous Valkyries. On that point I must admit the Captain's report had me stumped. But there could be an explanation, Sir; parachutes - giant cones of silk that can be strapped to a pilot's back. They are nothing new. Leonardo da Vinci had the idea first, but we've been testing designs with our balloon observers and with some success, give or take a few bumps and bruises.'

The Prime Minister shivered. 'Are you saying that these so-called flying women were exactly that... flying?'

'Not flying, more like floating to the ground. But what they jumped from, that's the important question, and there can only be one possible explanation - an airship.'

'And no one saw it in the sky?' asked the Prime Minister searching frantically through the pages of the report.

'The first time these women were seen 'flying' was at night. You have the photograph as evidence. On the second it was the following day. There was a low cloud cover over the moor.'

The Prime Minister slammed his fist down hard on the table. 'This is outrageous...'

'It is merely a suggestion.'

'Suggestion, be damned! It doesn't take an idiot to put two and two together and come up with war. It's a bloody certainty. That damned Kaiser's being playing us for fools, sailing his yacht in the channel and sipping cocktails with the

King. And why haven't we come up with something similar? Where are our airships, our planes, our own parachute troops?'

One of the grey-suited gentlemen coughed. 'Because we don't need them Prime Minister, we have the Navy.'

'Pah! A fat use they're going to be. What's the point in playing battleships if the blighters are dropping in on us unannounced? It seems we owe you an apology, Captain. You have shown us to be unprepared. These are dangerous times, too dangerous to sit back and do nothing. Have you any suggestions, Mr Jennings?'

'Only one at the moment, arrest the women.'

'Exactly, we can't have foreign agents spreading treason and gossip like a load of old fishwives. See to it will you Captain? You have my full support. Make a big show of rounding them up. There's no point in being secretive, the sooner the British public see the suffragettes for what they are, the better.'

The dawn chorus began in earnest, a crack of a shotgun and the clamour of startled crows, for the cook was laying in stores for the weekend and had chanced upon a recipe for birds nest soup. The sudden noise echoed around the school grounds, and in the boy's dormitory gummy eyes peeled open and tired heads shook themselves free from frosted pillows. Winter mornings were ever like this, a dull re-awakening to a cold slate floor, and the still sleepy shuffle to a bucket in the corner.

'Wassa-time?' asked a muffled voice from the tight wrappings of his grey blanket. A mittened hand reached out from the adjacent bed and fumbled for a clock, a battered tin object with only the hour hand attached.

'Sixes and sevens,' was the automatic reply.

'Too bloody early,' muttered the muffled voice and the boy turned over in disgust and tried to get back to sleep. But sleep

133

was impossible that morning, a cold wind struck up and whistled its way in through the gaps in the brickwork, stirring the atmosphere inside the room like a large wooden spoon. A few sensitive souls began to notice the difference.

'Bleugh! Who's left the lid off the bucket?'

'Shut up Mildew.'

'Well someone has, it reeks like a pigsty in here.'

'Then don't breathe in.'

'It's alright for you,' mumbled the delicate child. 'You've got a cold.'

Squint raised his head off the pillow and threw in his two-penneth worth. 'Bede!' he shouted. 'Are you awake?'

At the opposite end of the room, a tussle of red hair moved under a thin dirty sheet.

'Come on Bede, answer me.'

A pair of brown eyes flashed briefly open and stared angrily at Squint.

'Slop duty, and be quick about it!'

'Yeah come on Bede, we're being poisoned in 'ere!'

Bede swore under his breath and made a great show of burying himself under the covers.

'Blimey, did his Royal Highness use a dirty word?'

Squint rolled over on his back. 'Do you know Pursglove,' he said in a croquet and Pimms voice, 'I rather think he did.'

'Shocking…'

'Scandalous…'

'What has the upper crust come to?'

Someone threw a boot at Bede's bed.

'Careful, don't kick the bucket!' It was an old joke, but then there was little to laugh at in Grubdale Towers. Everyone thought it hilarious except for Bede. He threw off his sheet and sat up, his face tight with rage. 'You're all pathetic!' he said as he pulled his coat over his pyjamas. Squint bridled at the insult. 'Stop complaining and take the bucket outside,' he said, 'and for pity's sake be quiet. Some of us are trying to sleep.'

Poor Bede, fate had shaken him by the ears and acclaimed him a prince but had mislaid the trimmings, and what use was a royal title in a school like this? It had been a painful lesson. Instead of heeding Miss Carp's advice and keeping his mouth shut, Bede had boasted of his royal pedigree till the dormitory was a hot bed of Republican dissent. Royalty it seemed counted for very little. Instead of enjoying the fruits of privilege Bede was the butt of all jokes and the school whipping boy. Not that he had been popular before, but now his life was a misery. Damn Miss Carp and her empty promises. She'd said the bullying would stop. He sniffed back a tear of self-pity and dragged the overflowing bucket outside, making sure that none of its foul contents spilled on his feet.

'Were you born in a barn?' Squint called out at the top of his voice. 'Shut the flamin' door!'

Bede ignored the taunt and emptied the bucket noisily down the drain.

'A good morning for the exercise, yes?' shouted a voice in the distance. Bede turned around and saw from the light of the kitchen window the figure of a man in long football shorts and a knitted sweater running on the spot and swinging his arms to and fro.

'Tomorrow I get you all to do this.'

Bede was about to shake his head when he received a clout on the ear.

'I thought I told you to shut the door!' hissed Squint standing behind with a blanket wrapped around his shoulders. Bede mumbled an apology and ducked his head as Squint made to hit him again.

'Who's the idiot on the lawn?'

'I dunno, the new gym teacher I suppose.'

'I thought we'd seen the last of them.'

They both stood for a while, intrigued by the athlete's performance.

'He's a bit keen, stretching at this hour of the morning.'

Bede grunted a reply.

'What's he doing now?'

'Push-ups, I think.'

'There's no way he's getting me to do that.'

The two boys were not the only audience. From a window high up in the North Tower a telescope was bobbing up and down in time to the exercise.

'Look what's arrived in the morning post,' cooed Rowena admiring the scenery on the back lawn, and thinking how nice it would be to have hair like Rapunzel. 'Quite the Prince Charming and no mistake.' She risked a hearty 'good morning' and the cook swore as the rooks took fright and flew off to the next field. The athlete looked up to see where the voice had come from and noticed Rowena's window and the outline of something large and feminine wagging its fingertips daintily at him. He leapt to his feet and stood with his hands on his hips, swinging his body from side to side, a half-smile twisted on his face. So that is where the English Frauline is sleeping, he thought and made a mental note of the room's location, but his calculations were complicated by the sudden appearance of another woman at a window further down the tower. 'Good morning ladies!' he laughed. 'You will join me on the lawn, yes?' Rowena needed no encouragement, but Private Oldfield jumped back from the window and crouched down below the sill. There was no mistaking the man. It was that damned

136

German agent who'd attacked him with the bucket. Things were getting a little too hot for comfort at Grubdale Towers.

The backdoor of the school flung open and an excited Rowena dressed in wellington boots, her best nightdress and a dressing gown that billowed in the morning breeze like a sail on a galleon, jogged down the steps and across to the new gym teacher. Her cheeks were flushed with hastily applied rouge. 'It's so nice to find a kindred spirit. I often exercise in the morning before breakfast,' she lied as she skipped back and forth, dodging the man's swinging arms as he looked on in amusement. 'I'm Rowena Carp, by the way. I take the boys for Science.'

'Hans Bombast. It's my first day.'

'Well, hello Hans,' she giggled.

There was a yelp and an angry bark as Rowena stood back on Demetrios' paw. She used the stumble as an excuse to stop. 'Silly dog,' she laughed, 'always getting under my feet.' The look on Demetrios' face said a thousand words all beginning with the letter 'F'.

'No, no, keep going, Miss Rowena. Do what I am doing, yes?'

Rowena was a keen pupil and copied his exercises in a frightening display of unrestrained cotton and silk.

'It is good for the chest muscles you will find.'

Rowena fluttered her eyelids unashamedly and increased the tempo, any faster, and she would have started a fire. Their fingers touched.

'Perhaps we should stop the 'side to sides' and go on to the 'ups and downs?''

'Why not,' gasped Rowena. 'Oh, you mean touching the toes?' she added as Herr Bombast's face disappeared between his legs. 'I'll give it a go, but I can't promise success.' There was a creak of whalebone and stitching. 'Perhaps I'll just run around on all fours,' she whispered through clenched teeth as she felt something give way around her middle. 'It's good for the calf muscles.'

'You will do for your back an injury. Here, I take your hand and pull you upwards.'

Rowena accepted the gentleman's help and managed to stand up straight.

'So, we run around the school grounds, then a cold shower and breakfast?'

Any sense Rowena had when rushing down the stairs was now completely forgotten. 'That would be nice,' she said and trying to keep her corset from slipping down any further, she set off after the gorgeous young man as fast as her baggy boots would allow.

Squint watched the two figures run off into the shadows and cuffed Bede around the ear from sheer frustration.

'What was that for?' Bede complained.

'Shut up and get out of the way,' Squint said pushing the boy aside. Jealousy was a new emotion for him and came without instructions.

Anyone walking past the door of Hildegard Brent's room would have been forgiven for thinking she had a gentleman visitor and an excitable one at that, for Private Oldfield was talking to himself as he threw his belongings in his suitcase. 'Think Reginald, think,' he muttered as he sat down on the case and tried to shut the lid. 'What would the Captain do?' He decided upon the window and taking one last look around the room hitched his skirt to his knees and climbed on the bed. At least there was no one on the back lawn to see him escape, but oh dear, what a terrible long drop to the ground. There was only one choice; he would have to drag the luggage down the front stairs and brave it out with the headmaster. He sat down and tried to think of a suitable excuse, deciding against the obvious choice of blaming the cook. He pondered the problem some more then attacked his grey wig with his fingernails and rubbed his eyes until they were red and tearful. It would have to be a letter from a dying grandmother, an urgent request to return home. No, better make that a brother, he thought after looking at his reflection in the mirror. Any grandmother of Hildegard Brent's would be well beyond help.

Private Oldfield dabbed some water on his cheeks, then holding a handkerchief to his face opened the door to his room and dragged the suitcase after him, sobbing loudly for effect. No one was outside, so he pushed the luggage down the set of winding stairs and dashed along after.

'YOU!' cried a voice full of menace as he reached the bottom landing, for gravity had conspired to knock a certain Herr Bombast off his feet - gravity and a certain leather suitcase hitting the man squarely in the chest. There was an alarming note of recognition in his voice.

'I d-do apologise, the handle slipped out of my hand,' Private Oldfield stuttered trying to maintain the appearance of a grieving sister, but so had his wig. He hastily re-arranged the mop of grey hair as the prostrate German flung the luggage aside and struggled to his feet.

'You I remember,' Herr Bombast said shaking his finger as though it were a weapon. 'The Alpine Palace...'

'You must be thinking of someone else,' Private Oldfield insisted. 'Please step aside. I'm in a hurry. I have a brother dying of presumption.'

Herr Bombast put out his hand and held Private Oldfield back. 'You have been following me since the Hotel,' he said.

'I'm sure I don't know what you mean, now please let me pass.'

Herr Bombast prodded Private Oldfield painfully in the chest. 'Don't take me for a fool.'

'I beg your pardon?'

'I know who you are.'

'Of course you do. I'm Hildegard Brent.'

'A funny name for a cleaner of windows – or is it a waiter? No let me guess…' Herr Bombast flicked the wig from Private Oldfield's head as though it were a bluebottle on a piece of fruit. '…a man in a dress in a school for boys. Not your best work my English friend.'

Private Oldfield stepped back and looked up and down at the German. 'I could say the same for you, dolled up as a footballer with your shorts on back to front.'

'But at least they are trousers, yes?'

'You filthy German spy.'

Herr Bombast shook his head as though he was shocked to hear such language then struck out with his fist catching Private Oldfield squarely on the chin. The unfortunate victim's legs began to wobble before giving way underneath.

'Good morning Dr Brent,' mumbled Mr Gartside from the hallway as he shuffled his way along to the dining hall for breakfast, oblivious to the fact that the music teacher had fallen on her backside and that some strange gentleman was standing over her with his fist raised. Herr Bombast turned his head in puzzlement, distracted by the sudden appearance of the old gentleman and felt a stab of intense pain in his leg.

'You even fight like a woman!' he hissed as Private Oldfield withdrew the hatpin and struck again.

'Ah, Herr Bombast, I hope you slept well? Breakfast is at eight sharp although there is much to be said for arriving late,

140

if not at all.' It was the headmaster calling from below as he swept out of his office. He stopped for a brief moment at the foot of the stairs, then shrugged his shoulders and followed on after old Mr Gartside. 'Excellent, most excellent,' he said waving his hand in the air as a farewell gesture. 'The Sailor's Hornpipe – I'm sure the boys will approve.'

Whether they would or not, was the last thing on Herr Bombast's mind as he hopped around the stairs, trying to dodge the thrusts of the hatpin. He had heard of such weapons before, dipped in poison like a pygmy's dart and buried to the hilt in some unfortunate person's buttock. He kicked out with his foot, but felt it slip between the bars of the stair rail causing him to fall backwards on top of his opponent. He waited for the inevitable pain of the needle piercing through his shorts, but felt a warm gust of air as Private Oldfield spluttered and tried to get his breath. 'Did I hurt you?' he mocked then struck him in the stomach and snatched the pin out of his hand. 'Now tell me – why I am being followed?'

'But it's you that's following me!' hissed Private Oldfield.

'It's true, you are interesting – but more so the women, I think.' He leant his head close and whispered into Private Oldfield's ear. 'We know about the flying machine. Did you really think you could keep it a secret?'

Private Oldfield bit his lip. He would have to be careful what he said. The German was fishing for detail. 'I haven't a clue what you're talking about,' he said.

'Always the little games. What is it to be – you talk now, or I take you to my room?'

Private Oldfield knew only too well what such words meant. A crash course in interrogation had taught him all the horrors a private room could offer, including the tools.

Gathering all his strength he thrust upwards with his stomach and threw the German off to the side, then rolling on top he began to bang Herr Bombast's head against the floor. A surprised Rufus Doggerel tried to squeeze past on the stairs. 'My but you're a game old girl,' he said stepping over the music teacher. He winked at the face of the young man underneath. 'A whiff of the Amazon about our Dr Brent,' he quipped, but perhaps too much, he thought and tried to avert his eyes. He left the two 'lovers' canoodling behind and hurried off down the stairs as an out of breath Miss Carp and a panting Demetrios stumbled in from the outside.

Rowena closed the door and leant back on the wooden timbers, exhausted. 'Phew!' she gasped, wiping the sweat from her eyes with her sleeve. 'Not I think one of my better ideas.' Demetrios seemed to agree, his chest heaving like a pair of bellows, and his tongue nearly touching the floor. 'If ever I suggest running around the garden again, then just bite me hard on the ankle. You have my permission.' Rowena lowered her arm from her face and noticed an amused Rufus Doggerel smiling at her from the corner of the hall. Her demeanour changed at once. 'You can't beat a quick trot around the grounds for building up an appetite,' she said, thinking exactly the opposite. 'You should try it, Rufus dear. Blow those fusty old cobwebs away.'

Mr Doggerel looked unimpressed. 'I like my cobwebs exactly where they are, thank you very much. And please do up your robe. You look like a garden statue dragged in from the cold.'

Rowena ignored the insult and flounced across the hall, only to be steered in the opposite direction by a tactful pull on her sleeve.

'It looks as though Squint isn't the only one who needs a dose of your powders,' Mr Doggerel said, indicating with a quick movement of his eyes that something peculiar was going on behind.

'What on earth do you mean?'

'The old trout Hildegard, her sap has finally risen.'

'Really?' asked Rowena turning her head around. 'Where?'

'Don't make it obvious!' Mr Doggerel whispered enjoying the scandal. 'Up on the stairs to the left of the rubber plant. See, she has some poor young thing pinned down on the carpet.' Mr Doggerel was going to add something more, about the times we live in and the ever-creeping influence of the Pankhurst woman, when Rowena snatched her arm away and marched off to investigate. The old trout doesn't miss a trick, she thought. Hardly a night in the school and poor Hans is being tampered with. 'Dr Brent!' she shouted. 'What in heaven's name are you doing?'

Poor Private Oldfield, just as he was raising the suitcase over the German's head, the horrid Valkyrie of a woman rushed up from behind, dragged him backwards by the ears then struck him such a blow on the side of his head that he found it difficult to focus. Was he hearing correctly or had the woman just called him a dried-up prune, and, after picking up his grey wig from the floor, a filthy pervert? Whatever she said, there was no way the two of them were going to drag him away for questioning. He grabbed the suitcase to his chest and staggered to his feet, then with grim determination flung it in the direction of the woman.

'You unspeakable animal!' Rowena shouted as Private Oldfield ran down the stairs and fled out the front door. 'Rufus, are you just going to stand there? Get after that man and drag him back!'

143

Mr Doggerel was confused. 'What man?' he asked.

'Dr Brent of course!' Rowena screamed holding up the wig as evidence. 'Is there no vetting of staff in this establishment?'

'My dear Rowena, I draw the line at chasing after men, particularly those in skirts. What do you suppose I do if I caught one, talk about the weather?' But Rowena was not to be argued with. Her expression was set in stone and from what Mr Doggerel had just seen she had a persuasive right hook that could stop a steam locomotive. 'Oh very well, if you insist,' he moaned, and not exactly champing at the bit, Rufus flung open the front door and slouched away after the peculiar Hildegard.

Rowena's expression softened as she bent down and helped the stunned Herr Bombast to his feet. 'What must you think of us,' she said as she guided him upstairs, 'harbouring a pervert and not knowing the difference.' She leant her head close. 'I for one am all woman,' she whispered, 'in case you're worried.'

Herr Bombast groaned and put a hand to his aching head.

'There, there,' Rowena cooed, steering him in the general direction of her room. 'You mustn't worry. You're no less a man for a little tinkering with. Put it to the back of your mind and file it away as experience. This is England and we must make allowances.'

The confused and concussed Herr Bombast found himself being rushed into a strange bedroom and dumped unceremoniously onto a chair. This was not how he had planned the interrogation. It should have been the woman in the chair and himself striding about the room. With an increasing sense of danger he watched as Rowena locked the door and placed the key in the pocket of her dressing gown.

'Now let's see to that head of yours,' he heard her say. 'I'm sure I felt a bump.'

Rowena kicked off her wellingtons and set to work massaging the young man's scalp, gently at first but as her mind began to wander across the Scottish glens, her fingers were lost in a frenzy of plucking sprigs of heather from the turf.

'Ouch!' Herr Bombast complained as his head bent back over the sink.

'Oh do shut up Angus, and go with the flow,' teased Rowena before realising what she was doing. She opened her eyes and restored the young man's hairstyle to an acceptable shape. Something brushed her kneecap. 'Hans Bombast!' she giggled and tweaked his nose. 'Is that a pistol in your pocket?' But unfortunately for Rowena it was. The man took out the gun and pressed the barrel hard against her stomach.

'You will step away and sit down on the bed,' Herr Bombast said, and Rowena did as she was told. There was something insulting in the look of fear in his eyes.

'You scare easily,' she complained.

'Please, you will be quiet. I need to think. And the dressing gown, you will close it, yes?'

Rowena frowned. This was the second time her robe had been mentioned. Talk about making a woman feel unattractive. She folded her arms and stared angrily at her captor, as Herr Bombast stood up from the chair and walked to the safety of the other side of the room. 'Is the gun necessary?' she snapped. 'I think you've made your point.'

'I asked you to be quiet!'

'Fine, suit yourself.'

'Your performance on the stairs, Miss Carp; I must congratulate you. It was almost believable. Your companion in the dress, he has gone for help. That is clear to me.'

'He needs help…'

'Silence!' said Herr Bombast and glanced quickly out of the window. 'There is a back way out of the school, yes?'

Rowena refused to answer.

'I saw something like it when we were on the lawn.'

'Then why ask…'

Herr Bombast opened the door of the wardrobe and flung some clothes on the bed. 'You will get dressed Miss Carp, and please hurry. I can't afford to wait.'

'Then turn your head away.'

Rowena struggled into one of her dresses, pulling it over her night gown. 'Well then, what next?' she asked as her head emerged from the top.

'Now we will walk calmly out of the school.'

'We'll do no such thing. I have a class in one hour.'

'Miss Carp, you do not seem to realise. This pretence as a teacher is over. Now please hurry, I need to leave this place before the police arrive.'

Rowena's mouth went dry. This was the last thing she had expected, to be captured by one of Spleen's spies at the school. She tried to put on a brave face. 'Then you must also know that what you ask is impossible. I can't let you take me prisoner.'

'I have a gun Miss Carp. What do you intend to do – fight me for it?'

There was a noise from outside as someone turned the door handle. Herr Bombast put his finger to his lips. 'Shh!' he said, keeping the pistol aimed at Rowena. The door handle turned again.

'Miss Carp, are you there?' whispered a familiar voice.

'Damn it Squint, what is it with you and my bedroom?'

'That was a stupid thing to do,' Herr Bombast whispered. He caught hold of Rowena rudely by the arm. 'You will unlock the door and tell the person to go away. I shall be standing to your side so I can hear what you say.'

'Then get me the key. It's in my dressing gown,' Rowena whispered in reply. The door handle rattled as Squint tried it again. 'I need to see you Miss, it's important.'

Herr Bombast fumbled in the pocket of the dressing gown and pulled out the key. He was about to pass it to Rowena when with a flash of purple light, he found he had grasped a small ball of sharp metal spikes. He cried out in pain and tried to shake the object from his hand.

'What was that noise?' Squint shouted. 'Have you someone in there?'

Rowena ignored the disturbing implications of the comment and looked straight at Herr Bombast. 'I'm not sure,' she said. 'I'll tell you in a minute.' She stamped down hard on the young man's foot and grabbed at the pistol. There was a loud bang and a crash as the gun went off and the small sink exploded into fragments.

'I'm coming in!'

'No Squint, stay away from the door!'

Rowena struggled with the gun and tried to point the barrel away from her face and towards the window, but the German was too strong. He wrenched the pistol away and swung it round at her head. There was another flash of light and Herr Bombast found himself alone in the room. The lock to the door shattered with a kick from Squint and before the German could step out of the way, the door slammed open and knocked him off his feet.

'Miss Carp? Are you there?' asked an uncertain Squint poking his head around. A hand grabbed him by the shoulder and pulled him back on the landing.

'That's for the underwear,' Rowena said as she clipped him around the ear. 'Don't you do anything you're told? You could have been hurt.'

'But I thought you were in your room.'

'Well, you know what thought did. Now stay where you are while I go and get something.'

Rowena disappeared into the bedroom and dragged the unconscious Herr Bombast out by his feet. Squint stared aghast, his opinion of the lady increasing by the moment.

'Blimey Miss, what have you done to him?'

'Let's say the gentleman was foolish, and leave it at that. Go and find something I can tie him up with, and ask Mr Withers to call the police.'

Squint looked uneasy. 'I don't know about that Miss. Mr Withers ain't too fond of the police. I think this looks more like a job for The Firm.'

'Don't be silly and do as you're told.'

'He's not going to be happy about it.'

'Neither am I.'

Herr Bombast's eyes flickered open, but with a quick tap of the gun Rowena sent the poor man back into a comfortable sleep. 'By the way, what did you need to see me about?' she asked putting the pistol in her pocket. 'You said it was urgent?'

'Oh yeah, I forgot. It's about Bede. The stupid bugger's climbed on top of the roof and is threatening to jump off.'

Chapter Eight

The giant wyrm hovered high above Crewe station, out of sight from the people below. It had been a long and exhausting day carrying the two passengers on her back, and once or twice during their trip she had heard munching of sandwiches and the squeak of a thermos flask being opened from behind. She tried not to think of her stomach, but now late in the evening and with the night air thick with the smell of fried fish and vinegary chips, her mouth began to drool. Professor Broadbent leant forward and stretched out his arm as far as it would go, trying to sponge the creature's lips with his handkerchief.

'Do you want to get yourself killed?' Arabella asked, pulling him back by the shoulders. 'We're not flying high enough to risk swooping down and catching you if you slip. Stop fidgeting and sit still.'

The professor shook off Arabella's grasp and rearranged his scarf, but not before taking a tight hold of the wyrm with his knees. 'It may have escaped your attention Miss Pike, but Her Majesty is hungry,' he explained, feeling his authority being brought into question. 'I was attempting to prevent a waterfall.

If anything is certain to make those people down there look up, it's a bathtub of dribble landing on their heads.'

'Then I suggest the sooner we find this village the better.'

The professor ignored the comment and looked at his pocket watch. To continue the conversation was pointless, leading as it inevitably would to the subject of maps and how surprisingly difficult they were for men to understand. 'Any moment now,' he said, and as if on cue the night train to Holyhead blew its whistle and began to pull slowly out of the station.

'Are you sure that's our train?' asked Arabella.

'I'm positive Miss Pike, and nearly to the second.' The professor snapped his watch shut and placed it back in his pocket. 'Well?' he asked, turning around to look at his companion. 'Seeing as though the train was your idea, would you like to do the honours?'

Arabella smiled and nodded her head. 'Forward!' she shouted.

'Would you mind not digging your heels in,' cried the wyrm. 'A simple tap on the shoulder would suffice.'

'And remember, Your Majesty,' the professor added. 'Fly high and a little to the rear, but try and keep the glow from the firebox in sight.'

'And watch out for tunnels,' interrupted Arabella. 'You'll have to fly through those.'

'Is that wise?' the professor whispered. 'Surely it would be better to fly over them?'

'And run the risk of losing the train? How could we follow the tracks in the dark? We can't afford to be lost in the Welsh countryside for a fifth time.'

'Third, actually,' corrected Professor Broadbent then bent down as the wyrm gathered speed, his mind racing with images of low brick ceilings and heads being knocked backwards. He was wise to be cautious. The tunnels were hardly a wingspan across, yet far too long to enable the wyrm to glide through to the other side, and following the creature's first attempt Arabella began to doubt her own advice. The wyrm had swept through the opening and after tripping over the sleepers, had scrambled after the disappearing train like an old maid in a long skirt trying to catch a cyclist. Worse was to follow. At the second tunnel, the creature had taken hold of the brake coach with her teeth. After a sudden heart-stopping acceleration, it was decided that 'over hill' was better than 'under hill', and that perhaps on this point the Professor knew best. But Her Majesty was of a different mind. There had been too much flying, too little rest and not enough chewing of sheep. If people could hitch a lift on her back, then it was only fair that she could do the same. So, with little thought for the safety of her passengers, she chose the most comfortable of the carriage roofs and fell asleep with her wings tucked tightly into her sides.

If only she had chosen a carriage further back from the front of the engine. By Chester, the professor had started to cough and by Prestatyn he was beginning to fell distinctly unwell, but as the train pulled into Colwyn Bay, he was a converted smoker and gasping for a cheroot. At least the three were camouflaged against the night, their clothes and skin as black as soot and despite a narrow escape at Llandudno Junction where the wyrm had woken up with a dry throat, and had insisted on taking a drink from a water tower, their journey to North Wales had passed undiscovered.

'Time to get off,' Arabella said and roused the sleeping wyrm with yet another dig in her sides. 'This is as far as we go tonight. The Professor and I need some rest.'

Her Majesty yawned, swallowed a chimney full of smoke and stretched out her wings. 'And where should I take you now?' she asked sarcastically.

'Somewhere comfortable and out of sight if you don't mind,' said Arabella. 'And preferably clean.' The wyrm knew just the place and steered towards the sound of waves lapping over a shingle shore.

'And dry!' the professor shouted, but far too late. The wyrm had decided to take Arabella at her word and where else was cosier or out of sight than at the bottom of the sea, nestled in the soft mud.

It was as though anyone who spoke English was locked indoors.

'This is intolerable,' complained Professor Broadbent walking up and down the pier at Bangor harbour and asking the locals for directions. 'There must be someone who knows where this village is.' Armed with a past edition of the Bangor Herald the poor man had been slaughtering the Welsh language by asking anyone who walked past the whereabouts of Cloggy-noggy-whatever-you-call-it.

'You could try being polite,' suggested Arabella.

'Politeness be damned!' the professor said. He was not in the best of humour. Despite a spell or two from Arabella, his clothes were still damp from his dip in the sea, and now they smelled of something dead at the bottom of a rock pool.

'Perhaps you should give the newspaper to me. You look far too suspicious in your present state.'

'I hardly think that matters, Miss Pike. We face a conspiracy of misunderstanding. My pronunciation may not be perfect, but there can hardly be two places around here that begin with the letter C and last a lungful. No Miss Pike, we are being deliberately obstructed by grammar.'

'All the same, I think it would be best. At the very least I look less English.'

The professor snorted in anger and slapped the newspaper down into Arabella's outstretched hand. 'Have it your way. But I tell you, it'll make no difference.'

Arabella accepted the challenge and much to the professor's consternation walked up to a kiosk and bought a postcard. 'There, you see,' she said giving the card to the professor, 'Cloggy-noggy-whatever-you-call-it.'

On the front of the card were printed views of the village, including one of a large cave in front of a lake, and another of a very severe looking lady in national costume thinking very severe thoughts while gutting a fish.

'I asked the nice gentleman in the kiosk how to get to the village, and apparently it's only a few miles back along the main road.'

'I thought you couldn't speak Welsh' Professor Broadbent said.

'I can't, the gentleman was from Birmingham although I hardly understood a word.'

The professor was too annoyed to think of anything further to say, although as Arabella pointed out as she steered him in the direction of a café across the street, a thank you would have been nice. 'We deserve a slap-up meal after our little adventure,' she said as she opened the door and pushed him in.

The two of them sat at a table nearest the main window, and gazed out over the harbour. A shrill wind blew the tops of the waves white. In the distance they could see the grey-green

153

outline of Anglesey faded in the autumn sky, and a score of little boats tacking this way and that across the bay.

'A delightful place for a holiday. Quite a change from our gritstone and peat. Why, I'd say the place is almost Mediterranean in the summer.'

'I wouldn't be sure; too many snowstorms on sale in that kiosk for my liking. Still, I did see a palm tree on our way in, even if it was bent double by the wind.'

'I used to like fishing,' the professor said, referring to a small group of anglers casting their lines over the harbour wall. 'An enjoyable way to spend an afternoon. I was never any good, but that never seemed to spoil the fun. The pleasure was sitting down and falling asleep. I may take it up again when our troubles are over. Who knows, my temper may improve.'

Arabella smiled. 'I should hope so, and to make sure I'll buy you a little fishing net from the kiosk.'

'I apologise, have I been that impossible?'

'Like Rowena's Demetrios snapping at my ankles. Come on Professor, I'm famished. Read the menu. I'm sure chocolate is the same in any language.'

'I advise caution, Miss Pike. The Welsh are fond of their seaweed.'

'And why ever not, as long as there's a lobster and six oysters on top.'

So the two spent an amusing five minutes debating the various possibilities printed on the menu, and were pleasantly surprised when what they ordered turned out to be nothing more adventurous than egg and chips.

'One cannot improve on simplicity, Miss Pike,' said the professor dipping a fat golden chip into his yolk and popping it in his mouth with obvious relish. 'Although I see you have

154

peas with yours.' He was about to call the waitress back and ask for the same, when he shivered with the cold.

'Are you feeling well?'

'I think I've caught a chill from these damp clothes. Perhaps when you've finished chasing those peas around your plate, you could cast another spell in my direction. Brrr...it's as though someone's walked over my grave.'

The professor stopped talking and stared past Arabella. For one brief moment he thought he saw a face at the window looking in.

'Don't tell me, someone out there has caught a big fish.'

'I'm sorry Miss Pike. What did you say?'

'You went all quiet on me. I suspected a fish.'

'Really, of doing what?'

Arabella sighed and continued with her meal. It was quite obvious the professor was in one of his distant moods and not listening to a word she was saying. But if only he would keep his legs still, they were shaking so much the table was beginning to rattle. What was he looking at? Arabella turned her head around to see for herself and felt a sudden breath of fetid, cold air hit her face. The sudden breeze startled her.

'You can feel it too, that we're been watched?' the professor said, grasping her arm.

Arabella brushed away the professor's hand and tried to appear calm. 'Don't be silly, of course people are watching. We're strangers here. It's a small town.'

Professor Broadbent looked doubtful. Something peculiar was going on. He had seen a face pressed up against the glass, and not one you'd forget in a hurry, particularly if you'd been looking under the bed for some socks and it had brushed your hand with its chin. This was ridiculous. He was hallucinating from lack of sleep. But then why was someone breathing noisily in his ear? He turned his head to complain and something dark and shapeless flashed past his eyes.

'Please Professor, try and calm down. You're making me nervous with your endless twitching.'

The professor apologised and tried to sip his tea, but found his hands shaking so much that he dribbled most of it down his front.

'Congratulations,' Arabella said. 'Now everyone is looking.'

'Ssssh!' interrupted the professor placing the cup carefully back on the saucer and putting a finger to his ear. 'Can't you hear that noise, that slow, shallow breathing?'

'I hear nothing unless you mean the other people in the café.'

'I tell you Miss Pike, someone just blew in my ear.'

'Rubbish, it's just a draught. I felt it myself a minute ago.'

'And did it smell of mould or worse?'

'Maybe a hint of the grave, but that's hardly reason to act like a frightened rabbit. I expect it's the drains. We should have thought of that before. There was a perfectly good convenience on the pier.'

The professor wasn't listening. 'There's someone standing behind me. I can tell from your expression.' And before Arabella could shake her head the professor had banged his fists on the table and had twisted his chair around. 'Do you mind!' he shouted before realising there was no one there. The people in the café lowered their forks and stared open-mouthed, not a pretty sight with cabbage and bacon on the menu. Who did this stranger think he was, the King of bloody England? All the same, a few of them began to eat as quietly as their loose dentures would allow, and even went so far as to pour tea from their saucers back into their cups.

156

Professor Broadbent's face turned red with embarrassment. 'I'm terribly sorry,' he mumbled. He took a large silk handkerchief from his pocket and wiped the sweat from his brow. There could be no excuse. Here he was, a sensible man, twitching with adrenaline and acting as though someone had dropped a panic pill the size of a golf ball fizzing in his drink. 'Under the circumstances, Miss Pike,' he whispered. 'I think it would be best if we paid the bill and left. I'm not feeling the best.' But it wasn't Arabella who was sitting at the table. In her place sat a nightmare of a man, a tall, thin figure dressed in black, and with the face of a corpse and eyes of a dead herring far too long on the slab. 'Tell me where you've hidden the boy,' the strange man said, and the professor smelled mould and sour earth on the man's breath.

'I beg your pardon?'

'The boy, where is he? I need to know.'

'I'll tell you no s-such thing!'

'How very unwise.'

This was no temporary illusion. The stranger removed his mildewed top hat and shook his lank hair free. He picked up the menu and glanced at it briefly. 'What would you recommend?' he asked, and reaching out with his mottled hand poured more tea into the professor's cup. 'I expect the fish is good.'

Professor Broadbent was paralysed with fear. He could do nothing but stare as the spectre picked up a salt cellar and poured in three heaped spoonfuls before stirring the tea slowly with a chip from Arabella's plate. 'Drink,' the stranger said and sat back with folded arms. The professor shook his head.

'Not thirsty? Too much sugar perhaps. Now tell me, where is the boy?'

'I have n-no idea w-what you're talking about.'

'Oh, but I think you do. Drink your tea.'

It had been said so gently, not an order at all, but no matter how hard the professor tried to resist, he felt his own hand reaching for the cup and raising it to his lips.

'You are a weak man Professor, nothing more than a puppet. See how easy it is to pull your strings. I could make you slit your throat and smile at the privilege, but that would be a pointless exercise, not until you've told me the truth.' The stranger stabbed at the remains of a fried egg and the Professor watched horrified as the greasy yolk thickened and bubbled into the shape of a small chicken. The man grew bored and flicked the bundle of feathers across the table. 'You surprise me,' he said. 'Aren't you interested in who I am? I would have thought my appearance deserved comment. I prefer a simple honesty. Do you find my face hard to look at?'

The professor was struggling with his cup. 'I've seen worse,' he spluttered.

'I doubt that,' said the man peeling a nail from a finger. 'People call me The Undertaker, but then I think you know, don't you?'

The professor said nothing.

'Your silence is annoying, but of no consequence. You will tell me everything. How can you refuse? Wherever you are, then I will be...'

The glass thought the professor, how stupid of me to forget.

'Answer my question. Where can I find this boy?'

It was a battle of wills with the odds stacked in the Undertaker's favour, but the professor had a trick up his sleeve, or rather his jacket pocket. Of course he'd heard of the Undertaker, who hadn't? This was a creature of legend, a whispered threat in the ears of naughty children who wouldn't go to sleep. He bit on his tongue and remained silent.

'Are you trying to resist?'

The professor had managed to drop the cup and was reaching for a knife from the table.

'It won't do any good, you'll only cut yourself.'

The knife weighed heavy in his hands as though pulled by a magnet, but with all the strength he could muster Professor Broadbent pointed the blade at the stranger's chest. The Undertaker's face seemed to split in two as he smiled.

'Now you're being silly. Think, Professor - no blade could ever hurt me. You have to be alive to feel pain.'

The professor shook as he turned the blade on himself.

'I have underestimated you. So, the mirror is in your top pocket?'

The professor nodded.

'The ties that bind, how fragile they are. Bravo Professor, I shall not make the same mistake twice.'

'There will be no second time,' whispered the professor, and feeling the power of the Undertaker momentarily fail, he thrust the blade hard into his own chest. There was a spark and crackle of electricity, and the professor found himself staring once more at the friendly face of his companion, Miss Pike.

'You look as though you've seen a ghost,' said Arabella.

It took a few moments for the professor to gather his thoughts. 'My dear,' he said after reaching over the table cloth and drinking heavily from the milk jug. 'I've been very foolish.'

'You've been very messy, pouring tea down your front and dropping fried egg on the floor. And what was all that nonsense with the knife? You had me worried.'

The professor reached inside his jacket and brought out a small velvet bag. He shook its contents out on the table and stared at the broken remains of a small hand mirror, the face of the Undertaker peering out from each shard of glass before vanishing into the darkness.

Arabella drummed her fingers nervously on the table. 'I thought you told us to get rid of those damn things,' she said.

'I did, and I'm an idiot to have kept this. You asked me if I had seen a ghost, Miss Pike, and my answer is yes. That face you saw in the glass, it was the Undertaker.'

Arabella stood up from the table in alarm.

'You needn't worry, he's gone now; some trickery of the sorcerer no doubt. I've been stupid, Miss Pike and I apologise. By looking into the mirror I released a devil. Thank heavens the others are locked away in my office.'

'But can you be sure, I mean Professor...the Undertaker. What happens if they fall into the wrong hands?'

'Please, Miss Pike; trust me. As long as those mirrors are out of sight then we're safe. He can only get through if someone looks into the glass. I'll destroy them all when we get back home.'

Arabella's confidence was decidedly half-hearted. 'What's happened to our world, Professor? Are we to fight the dead as well as the living, what more tricks will Spleen throw at us?'

'Don't get cold feet, please, not you of all people.'

'Oh, I won't give in. I can't say the same about the others, though. Not when they hear about this.'

'Then we shall keep it a secret. Besides, it would appear we have a more urgent problem on our hands.'

'You mean?'

'Look out of the window, Miss Pike. I'm afraid Her Majesty may be causing trouble.'

Arabella gazed outside and groaned with disappointment. 'Not again,' she cried as each angler on the harbour wall turned a somersault in midair and fell in the water, for whatever bait they were using was as a plate of sausages to a hungry wyrm.

Miss Wallace rubbed the last smear of polish into the professor's desk and stepped back to admire her handiwork. She was a proud housekeeper and considered her elbow grease the best in Grubdale. Let the old codger complain about his room now, she thought. I've dusted each corner, thrashed each carpet and polished every surface till it shines, and trust the professor to be off gallivanting about the countryside now I've finished. She eyed the tantalus on the side table and licked her lips. Surely the odd glass or two wouldn't be missed,' she thought, seeing how good a job I've done. She rattled the top of the tantalus and swore under her breath. It was locked and for one good reason. Miss Wallace's idea of an odd glass or two would keep a bishop giggling for a month. The temptation was too much. 'Thinks he's got the better of me, does he,' she muttered. 'Well, I knows different. I knows where he keeps the key.' She knelt down in front of the desk and examined the lock of the wide front drawer.

'Pathetic, a Warpington and Stanley Number Eight. A baby could open one of these with a nappy pin.' But seeing as no baby was at hand, Miss Wallace pulled a hairpin from the back of her bonnet and twisted it into the keyhole.

'One click up, two clicks down and a fiddly bit in the middle. There we have it!'

She put the pin back behind her ear and slid the heavy drawer out with surprising ease. 'Oh my, isn't he the vain one,' she said, for stacked at the back of the drawer was a collection of silver hand mirrors. 'Blimey, look at the state of my face, there's muck everywhere.' She pulled a handkerchief from her sleeve and with the help of a little spit and dribble cleaned the smut away from her cheek. 'Now, there's beautiful...'

'You've missed a bit,' whispered a voice from behind. 'Here, let me help.' And the last thing Miss Wallace saw before leaving this world was a large wet flannel being pressed to her face.

The headmaster slammed the telephone receiver back on its hook and poured himself a large whisky from the hollow statue on his desk. He had just been called every adjective The Firm could think of with a few scurrilous nouns thrown in for good measure, the gist of the conversation being that some idiot in the school had called for the police.

'Impossible!' the headmaster had cried. 'No one here would be so stupid!' Yet according to The Firm's boss, Rabid O'Hooligan, a Black Maria with half a dozen of the toughest policemen on board had set off in the direction of Grubdale Towers. It was time to panic, but not before the headmaster had downed the last dregs from the statue and had replaced the head of John Wesley on backwards. He marched out of his office and ordered every boy he could get his hands on to hide the school silver, and every member of staff to throw their betting slips on the fire. 'We are about to be raided,' he warned. 'So man the barricades and leave the talking to me!' Rowena knew nothing of this being halfway up a drainpipe with her skirt caught on a nail.

'Bede!' she shouted. 'I'm getting tired of these games. What in heaven's name do you think you're doing, climbing on the roof and threatening to jump off? Have you lost your mind?'

A clump of moss torn from the slates flew past her shoulder.

'You lied to me!' cried Bede's voice. 'You promised the bullying would stop!'

'Is this what it's all about – a broken promise?' Rowena kicked her leg to dislodge the nail and felt the bottom of her skirt rip open. 'Well I'm sorry Bede, but I can't work miracles. You've hardly made yourself popular, and sulking won't help.'

Another clump of moss hurtled past her face.

'I'm not sulking!'

'Then would you please mind telling me what you are doing?'

Bede's face appeared over the guttering. It was obvious he'd been crying. 'I was waiting until you got here,' he said.

'Fine, then be a good sport and lend me a hand. This drainpipe's about to give way.'

It was not a graceful picture, Rowena trying to lift her leg over the edge of the guttering, while Bede pulled and tugged and hoisted her across. Despite the puffs and pants and expression on his face, Rowena was less than impressed with his efforts. She sat down exhausted on the slate roof and examined the rent in her skirt.

'I hope you're satisfied. I've a good mind to give you a slap.'

Rowena moistened her finger in her mouth and slid it along the tear, not caring if the boy saw the two ends of the fabric stitch themselves mysteriously together. 'Well then,' she said. 'Explain yourself!'

Bede looked carefully at the mended skirt. He'd remembered many things since their earlier conversation, the use of magic being foremost in his mind. 'I want to go home,' he mumbled and tried to cry some more. Rowena softened a little and put a friendly arm around his shoulder. My but the boy stinks, she thought, and made a mental note to pour an extra spoonful of sulphur in the bathtub that evening.

'Of course you want to go home. We all do. I promise you won't have to wait long. As soon as the Professor sends word we'll pack our bags and fly out of here.'

Bede raised his head and looked long and hard at Rowena. 'Fly?' he asked. Rowena wasn't sure she should have told him this. She shrugged her shoulders. 'In a manner of speaking, yes,' she said.

Bede pushed Rowena's arm away in a huff. 'I can't wait any longer. I want you to take me home now.'

'Don't be stupid, it's impossible.'

'But I order you to do it,' Bede shouted. 'I'm your King!'

It was hardly a convincing argument. Bede dressed in his dirty school clothes, wiping his nose on his sleeve and looking every inch a stranger to the nit nurse.

'A king is it? Why only yesterday you were happy being a prince.'

'Why shouldn't I be a king? My father's dead, you said so yourself. It's your duty to serve me.'

Rowena flinched. The boy did have a point, but a cold and ruthless point at that, and one not worth pressing considering his present mood. A consolatory gesture was needed before the situation got out of hand. Rowena tried to think of what Arabella would do, other than tying the ungrateful wretch in a sack and throwing him in a pond. 'Your Highness,' she said and patted his knee. 'Surely we can wait a few days, and if it would make you feel any better, I could arrange a trip to town. What would you say to a new set of clothes and some soap?'

Bede looked at her in puzzlement.

'And a haircut? We can't have a Prince of Wyrm looking like a common chimney sweep now, can we?'

As bribes went, it was a good deal short of thirty pieces of silver, not even a handful of coppers in Bede's mind. 'I am not a prince,' he insisted. 'I am your King!'

Rowena knew precisely what Arabella would have done, and rolled up her sleeves accordingly. 'That is for your people to decide, you heartless boy. A king must earn the right to his crown, and as far as my duty's concerned, I'll box your blasted ears!'

Bede scuttled out of harm's way. 'Stay where you are,' he said stepping back towards the guttering.

A number of boys stopped pushing their wheelbarrows stuffed high with school silver, and looked up at the roof. 'Isn't that hairy-arse?' they asked. They began to laugh and wave their arms. 'JUMP! JUMP!' they cried until quite a crowd had gathered on the lawn.

'You see!' Bede cried out in despair. 'They hate me!'

Rowena got to her feet and dusted her skirt. 'Now you're being silly,' she said, feeling her patience come to an end. 'They don't hate you. They think you're peculiar, and who can blame them? I told you to keep your identity secret, but would you listen? Oh no, his 'High and Mightiness' thought better of advice. Well, young man, you reap what you sow.'

Bede turned his back on Rowena and was stared at the chanting crowd. 'I'll teach you to laugh at a King!' he shouted and pulled a few loose slates from the roof, hurling them over the side.

'Stop that at once!' Rowena cried, and pulled the boy back by the scruff of his neck. She boxed him firmly around the ears. 'What do you think you're doing? You could kill someone!'

Bede struggled free. 'Don't you ever hit me again!' he shouted and stepped back to the edge of the roof. Rowena panicked.

'I'm sorry, I'm sorry. Arabella said I had a quick temper. Please, Your Highness, show some sense and move away from the edge. You could slip and fall and what use would you be then, all bent and broken like a rag doll.'

Bede tried to steady himself. 'Who is Arabella?' he asked, confused.

'She's another one of your guardians, and heaven help me if she saw you now. I'd be drummed out of the sisterhood if any harm came to you.'

Bede thought for a moment, then smiled. 'But no harm will come to me, not with you around.'

'Not if you step away. Now please Your Highness, walk to me.'

'Even if I did fall, I wouldn't hurt myself. You would see to that.'

'What do you mean?'

'I'm too important. You would have to catch me before I hit the ground.'

From the surprised look in Rowena's eyes, Bede knew it to be true. It had happened before, a long time ago, when he'd slipped and fallen from a nursery window - a distant memory of being swept up in a woman's arms, and flown high above the rooftops. He took a tentative step backwards. 'You will show them how important I am, and then the bullying will stop.'

'No, Your Highness, please, don't do it!'

Bede had made up his mind. If the school wouldn't believe him then his guardian, Miss Carp, would prove them wrong. He felt carefully with his foot and trod on nothing but air. For a brief second his eyes betrayed his fear, and then with a scream he toppled backwards and fell from view.

'Oh bugger!' Rowena swore, and in a blur of movement flew down after him.

It was difficult to say who was the most surprised, those pushing wheelbarrows on the lawn and seeing their science teacher sweep the falling Bede into her arms, or poor Rowena flying headlong into the side of the Black Maria as it pulled up on the gravel drive. She'd barely enough time to gather her senses and carry the boy back to the roof, before an excited Captain Dashing jumped out of the van. 'Did you see that!' he exclaimed, ushering the constables out through the back door and checking the scratched paintwork. 'A deliberate act of vandalism! What happened, did someone throw a stone?'

'Looks too big for a stone,' said one of the constables looking over the captain's shoulder. 'More like a sledge hammer.'

Captain Dashing eyed the crowd of boys with suspicion. 'Hooligans,' he muttered, removing his revolver from its holster. 'Right then gentlemen, truncheons at the ready and stay close to me. We're going to storm the front door.'

'Sir?'

'What is it constable, speak up.'

'Er…they're only boys. Is the gun necessary?'

'Of course it is man! Don't be fooled. Heaven knows what they're holding behind their backs.'

'But a gun, Sir?'

The captain looked the portly policeman up and down. 'I take it you weren't in the Sudan,' he said.

'Not me, Sir.'

'Exactly, just my point. When you've seen what I've seen, bleeding on the desert sand, then you'll learn to be more suspicious. You see this scar here?'

Captain Dashing pointed to a slight blemish on the side of his nose.

'Yes, Sir.'

'Need I say more?'

The constable wished he would, although the truth of the matter was less exciting – an over friendly camel on a dark night with the glow from a hookah behind it.

'All the same Sir, this is England.'

The captain dismissed the comment with a wave of his hand, and turned to face the crowd of boys. 'Listen here; we want no trouble so put down your weapons.'

The boys looked at each other in confusion, what could this strange man mean?

'Come on, slowly now,' said the captain waving the revolver in their direction. 'No sudden movements.'

The boys let their wheelbarrows drop to the ground and Pursglove, in a state of fright, put his hands up in the air.

'Good, that wasn't so difficult now, was it? Constable, if you please.'

'What?'

'The weapons man, get your colleagues to gather them up!'

'You mean the wheelbarrows?'

'If that's what you call them, then yes!'

The policemen stayed where they were and muttered amongst themselves. The captain was mad, they thought. It would be better bundling him into the van than any women. And what had their sergeant been thinking of allowing the army to take command?

A pistol fired and a policeman's helmet rolled along the gravel.

'You'll never take me alive!' shouted a voice from the roof and everyone dashed for cover. Rowena couldn't have chosen a worse time to raise her head above the guttering and shout 'Who said that?'

'You see!' the captain said, pointing excitedly at Miss Carp. 'There's your German spy!'

He was nearly correct, for the person who'd fired the shot was a confused and concussed Herr Bombast holding on to a chimney for support and thinking himself under siege.

The adventure continues in
'The Allure of the Red Wyrm'
The final part of 'The Trouble with Wyrms' trilogy

List of Characters

The Sisterhood – a once important guild of witches from the planet Vivarium, protectors of the exiled prince of Wyrm and now seekers of the giant wyrms of antiquity.

Arabella Pike – senior member of the Sisterhood and life-long companion of Rowena Carp with, as Arabella would be the first to admit, the mental scars to show for it. Perhaps the most serious member of the guild but that's not saying much. Lives in the village of Sodden-on-the-Bog and as our story begins has been excavating the cellars of her house to discover the source of a deep rumbling, snoring noise that keeps her awake at nights. She has been known to keep a cave squid or two in her cellar to deter burglars.

Rowena Carp – a flamboyant member of the Sisterhood given to pouncing on Scottish pipers and declaring her love. Life-long companion of Arabella Pike with, as Rowena would be the first to admit, the mental scars to show for it. She is the only member of the Sisterhood to keep a familiar, which in her case is a Jellico she discovered in a very cheap restaurant, lying on her salad and with an apple in its mouth. In remembrance of a past affair and of a similar posture, she has named the Jellico Demetrios.

Bethesda Chubb – the youngest member of the Sisterhood and the most erratic, given to fighting at the least opportunity and declaring her admiration for Emmeline Pankhurst and the Suffragettes. She is often found wearing a necklace of dentures – prizes from numerous encounters with the London constabulary – and a policeman's helmet. She is fond of any weapon that makes a loud noise and shreds her enemies to jam and biscuits.

Demetrios – a Jellico from the forests of Tweeb and beloved companion of Rowena Carp. Resembles a fat pink poodle but breathes fire and would bite the hand off your arm if you offered him a dog biscuit.

Professor Arbutus Broadbent – the only male member of the sisterhood on account of his very great intelligence and sobriety. Considers himself to be a man of science but is not averse to the odd spell or two, as long as he is looking the other way.

Miss Wallace – Professor Broadbent's house keeper of dubious history. She is rather fond of the Professor's sherry if only she could get her hands on the key to the tantalus.

Reverend Ainsley Cross – Vicar of the Parish of Sodden and keen amateur photographer. He likes nothing better than to drape his house cleaner in robes and flowers and make her 'smile at the birdie.' He has now fled the village after suffering a crisis of faith and is having another crisis of faith as to what to do with a large Gladstone bag stuffed to the handles with gold sovereigns.

Captain Hilary Dashing – Captain of the 1st Grubdale Rifles and erstwhile not-so-secret agent for the War Office.

Private William Oldfield – Private of the 1st Grubdale Rifles and erstwhile ever-so-not-so-secret agent for the War Office.

Herr Bombast – German spy with the unfortunate habit of bumping into Private Oldfield on a regular basis.

The Prime Minister – suspicious of Germany and the Suffragette movement in general.

Mr Jennings – a terribly clever man at the War Office.

Joseph Nadin – award-winning pork butcher and part-time taxi driver for Grubdale Towers. His sister is the school cook.

Darkly Withers – Headmaster of Grubdale Towers; a cold, sarcastic individual with a penchant for piranhas in the school pond.

Reginald Doggerel – English teacher at Grubdale Towers; a man of the world who having settled for life in a small northern town, is bored with his lot. He misses the green fingers of Mr Clitheroe and, in particular, the 'special stuff' he grew in the school greenhouse.

Mr Clitheroe – an ex-science teacher at Grubdale Towers. He was last seen being carried from the school after eating a tin of green sardines.

Jack Gammon – sports master and geography teacher at Grubdale Towers; fond of exercise, tattoos and little kittens in that order. His sheer presence is enough to quell any classroom riot but deep, deep down he has a soft heart...somewhere.

Mr Gartside – the eldest member of the teaching staff at Grubdale Towers. He takes the boys for classes in evaluation or, as Mr Doggerel explains, pricing the stolen silver.

Mr Maurice – an unfortunate music teacher at Grubdale Towers. He was last seen being carried from the school after eating a green meat pie.

The Cook – Mr Nadin's sister; a formidable woman with little sympathy for delicate stomachs and even less sympathy for Grubdale wildlife.

Matron – a mysterious character who treats all sick boys as though they were horses. She gets her pills and drenches at cost price from the local vet.

Mildew, Melor and Pursglove – pupils at Grubdale Towers

Squint – the eldest pupil at Grubdale Towers. If this were a private school in the south of England he would be Head Boy, but as it's a forgotten backwater of education in a small northern town, then he's just bigger and taller than the rest of the boys.

Hieronymous Bede – the Prince of Wyrm; rescued as a child and smuggled to Earth over ten years ago, Bede is unaware of his inheritance.

Tarantulus Spleen – terrifying Sorcerer and ruler of Vivarium, usurper of the Throne of Wyrm, murderer, card sharp and downright nasty person altogether.

Vermyn Stench – Head of Spleen's Secret Service - half man, half rat, all bad.

Serrin Gutterprod – Tarantulus Spleen's head torturer and wielder of the big syringe.

The Undertaker – a feared necromancer in league with Spleen.

The Blue Wyrm – one of the stately wyrms of England, an ancient race of dragons that have shaped the universe as we know it today, mostly by drilling wyrmholes in space and letting any old riff-raff through.

About the Author

Mike Williams (1959 to one day when he's not looking) was born in the town of Market Harborough and due to a mix up with a local fortune teller was photographed for much of his first year in a dress. After moving to the Derbyshire Dales to escape the shame, he took to farming like a duck to liver pate and for many years seemed perpetually doused in manure, mostly from slipping on the cobbles or walking too near the cows at milking time. Educated at Buxton College, Chesterfield Art College and Trent Polytechnic, he threw away the wellington boots for a briefcase, was awarded a doctorate in 1986 and since then has lectured and published widely in plant physiology. He can be found waxing lyrical to students on the intimate contents of a leaf at Trinity College, Dublin or running around a park in an attempt to lose weight. He is married with two goldfish and an overdraft.

Printed in Poland
by Amazon Fulfillment
Poland Sp. z o.o., Wrocław

54576547R00103